Dripping for Your Pleasure

Pleasure

Dirty Voyeurs Book 2

J. P. Newmon

J.P. Newmon

Contents

For the girls with a spooky lean

CONTENT WARNINGS

Dripping for Your Pleasure is an open-door, paranormal romance novel. It is book 2 in a standalone interconnected series. This content is intended for 18+ and includes references to the paranormal, violence, and erotic adult scenes. Please read at your own discretion.

INTRODUCTION

You've spent decades believing your fate was sealed. Doomed to spend eternity watching others live while you exist in isolation. Then chance brings someone who awakens hopes and dreams you thought were long buried. Can you break through the bonds of reality to reach her?

Willow Nightgood has always loved the dark and spooky, but none of that is real, right? When the mysterious happenings around her home and business finally get too blatant to ignore, she must come to terms with the reality of the supernatural. As the hauntings turn into cries for help from beyond, Willow is faced with a choice. As she strives to help her paranormal guest cross over, she finds herself falling for a man she can never truly have. Has she finally gotten in too deep with her love for the macabre, or could this be something more?

Chapter 1
Dead Man Walking

FUCK THIS JOB. I could have been a lawyer, you know. *We regret to inform you, Gerald, that you have failed to meet the academic requirements to continue in this program.* Fuck 'em all. I was smarter than all of them. I was gonna shake things up, but they couldn't handle it, so they screwed me over. Now, I'm in this fucking dead-end job. I take a long drag on my cigarette. The alley behind the building is fucking disgusting, but you can't smoke out front. There's litter, and it smells of rotting garbage from the dumpster where the restaurant next door dumps all its food waste.

I should be smoking nice cigars in a cushy office with a view. Not this fucking gig. I throw my cigarette down in a puddle next to my feet and press it with my shoe. The door pops open, and that bitch that sits in the cubicle next to me— I think her name is Debby, Deborah, Donna? I don't fucking know and don't fucking care, uppity cunt— pokes her head out into the alley. She always has this disgusted look on her face when she talks to me. Would it kill a bitch to smile once in a while?

"Gerald, Steve from HR is looking for you... again. He wants you to meet him in his office." She slams the door back, not waiting for any acknowledgement from me. I fucking hate that bitch. I fucking hate this job, but it won't be long. I'll get straight again soon, then this shit will be just a bad memory.

I open my phone again to check the messages my buddy sent me. There's a fight tonight, and if I want in, I need to transfer the money now. Shit, $3K? But I could win. I need a win. Betting against the favorite is riskier.

I scroll through the messages again.

> Ricky: Don't puss out. This is a sure thing. I know a guy who can get access to the locker room, he's gonna help us out, if ya know what I mean.

> Ricky: Come on, man…

Fuck. I need this. I could pay off a little of my debt.

> Me: Fine, I'm in. Send it to ya now.

I shove my phone back in my pocket. I need another cigarette, but there's no time. I'm already gonna catch shit for taking an extra break. The back door slams behind me as I step back into the building. I make my way through the sad hallways up to Steve's office. What the fuck does he want this time? Grey walls, grey linoleum, fluorescent lights with only half the bulbs working; fuck, could this place get any more depressing?

I don't even knock, just barge in and throw myself down in his chair. I'm in here so fucking much, maybe my name should be on the door. He's on the phone and looks up at me, exasperated. He can fuck off. He came looking for me. I should be at my cubicle doing the fucking shit they call work around here.

I drum my fingers on my knee while I wait for him to finish his phone call, fucking rude keeping me waiting. He thinks he's so much better than me. Always on me about my breaks, when I clock in and out, how many calls I log— blah blah blah "time theft." I'm one of the best workers they have here. They'd be fucking stupid to fire me.

The slam of the handset into the base brings my attention back to Steve. He's looking at me like he wants to throw me out of a window, his hands steepled at his chin. I guess that's supposed to intimidate me. Pause for dramatic effect— fucking clown.

"Gerald, there have been more complaints about the way you answer calls." He pauses. I know he's waiting for me to give something up, but I haven't done anything wrong. He straightens the wire-frame glasses on his fat nose, then lifts a stack of papers and taps them on the desk to even the edges out. I straighten myself in the cheap vinyl chair, bracing for whatever fucking nonsense he's about to spew at me.

"These are the transcribed records of several calls you've taken spanning over the last three months. Do you see how thick this stack is, Gerald? These are just the most egregious ones. I have every call you've taken. I pulled these to highlight as examples for *this* conversation. This presents a consistent pattern of behavior that is in opposition to our outlined code of ethics for this job."

Again, he pauses. I guess it's my turn. "Just words typed on a page aren't the whole picture, Steve, and you know that. You can't tell the tone of voice something was stated in, so it's basically all taken out of context and subject to bias based on the reader's opinion of me." I would've made a badass lawyer.

"Yes, Gerald, you have made that argument in the past. I don't think that holds up to you telling Mrs. Walters, "You stupid cunt. You need to learn how to fucking read the directions before you call up here and waste my fucking time. Go back to knitting your dead cat a sweater and stop calling customer service."

Fuck. We stare at each other, neither backing down. "Yeah, but somebody's gotta tell them like it is. This world is full of snowflakes who want to take advantage. I just saved the company probably $200 by not replacing that electric cooker, plus the shipping for the new one and the return of the old."

I sit back in the chair and cross my leg over my knee, a power move of body language to show my confidence, a total lawyer move. "It's stupid, she didn't read the user manual, and she thinks she needs a new one for free."

Steve sits back in his chair and sighs. "Gerald, the company expects to take some losses to keep customers happy and feeling like they are being valued. Customers who feel valued leave good product reviews. Good product reviews lead to increased sales. Customers who get cursed out on the customer service line leave negative reviews. Negative reviews hurt sales. So, it doesn't matter if you think you saved the company a few hundred dollars by pissing off a little old lady."

I roll my eyes, fuck this shit again about product reviews. "Gerald, are you listening? The company requires that I give you a probationary period to reform your work habits. For the next few months, you will have a supervisor listening in on all your calls. If you slip up again... I will fire you."

I let the door slam behind me on my way out of his office. So, what? He thinks he has me pinned down with that threat? When

Ricky comes through, I'll be the one walking out on this job. Then he can have the headache of trying to replace a solid worker. He'll see what kinda employee he drove off with his micromanaging.

"So, how was your talk with Steve?" The snooty crooning of that uppity cunt drifts over my shoulder as I'm stomping down the hall back to my cubicle.

"Fuck off, Deloris."

"Dina."

"I don't give a fuck what your name is, and what happens in HR is none of your goddamned business. So, stop being a nosy bitch." I snarl over my shoulder.

"Oh, sounds like it wasn't a great meeting, then. You mean he didn't kiss your ass and offer you a raise and a promotion?" she giggles.

I turn to face her. She folds her arms in front of her chest as she saunters closer, her cheap heels clicking obnoxiously on the hallway floor. I hope she gets hammer toes from wearing those stupid things. She leans in with a sneer curling her lips.

"I can't wait until they finally have enough of your shit and you get fired. I only hope I'm on the schedule that day so I can have a front row seat to you packing your stuff and getting the fuck out." She flips her hair over her shoulder and leaves me standing in the hallway.

I have to dig my fingernails into my palms to keep from reaching out and squeezing her neck. Fuck her. Fuck this job. Fuck all these people who think they're so much better. And fuck the phone lines. Instead of going back to my cubicle, I turn the corner at the end of the hall and head back to the alley. I need another cigarette.

The smell of soiled, dirty diapers and ammonia stings my eyes. I fucking hate this place. Cheapest I could find, though. My shoes squeak on the linoleum as I make my way down the hall. Even the nurses look like they came at a discount. Whatever happened to nurses being hot?

I turn the corner and see her sitting in the back corner of the game room, working on a puzzle. Her cane leaned up against the table, and the sleeves of that beige cardigan she always wears— a cardi, she'd always called it— catching puzzle pieces and knocking them on the floor. I pull up a chair and plop down at the table. "Hey," I say.

She looks up at me and smiles, no clue who I am. "Oh, hello. Are you wanting to do a puzzle? They have a wonderful selection right over there." She points toward a supply table set up along the wall. Her eyes come back to me, searching my face. It's been like this for a long time now. Her expression shows she knows she's probably supposed to know me, and using vague conversation to try and dance around the fact that she has no clue.

Confliction pulls at my chest. I squandered a lot in my early adult life. The debt from my wasted time in law school, the inheritance my parents gave me afterward so I could have seed money to get my life together— lost that in a pyramid scheme— and now I'm in even more trouble trying to gamble it all back.

I reach into my back pocket for my wallet and pull out a picture of the three of us from when I was a little boy. The photograph is a rosy sepia from age, and the edges crinkled from living in my wallet. I lay it flat on the table next to her puzzle and smooth it out with my thumbs. As usual, her face morphs from confusion to recognition to joy. "Oh! That's my Gerald! Do you know him? He's the sweetest little boy, but full of mischief... always finding a bit of trouble that one." She laughs fondly as she gently brushes the picture with her fingertips.

Emotion clogs my throat as I remember the good times, before life got so hard, and I was happy. Growing up, I was happy. Not weighed down with guilt and money problems. Back when I knew my parents were proud of me, not like my adult years.

"Yeah, I know him. Real good kid." She beams with pride. Not at all confused why this grown man, a stranger as far as she knows, is carrying around a picture of her little boy in his wallet.

Just like all our visits, I swallow my grief and guilt and lead her down a conversation, asking about his childhood and her life before, back in London. I listen for clues to anything that could be of value. My grandparents had given her this little oddities shop in London as consolation for their absence in her life while they traveled the world.

Growing up, I used to explore it all in the attic. Packed up after they fled London and the War. I was both intrigued and appalled at all the different trinkets and wares. There has to be something up there that's worth a shit ton of money. I got debt collectors on my back, and not the legit kind. I need big money, fast.

I always come up empty, though. Never any clues. I've hauled so much of that crap to antiques dealers, hoping to find something worth shit— always nothing. I'm always coming up with nothing.

Guilt churns my stomach at what she would think if she knew what I was really up to, why I stashed her in this shit hole facility and not something nicer. I fucking hate sitting here listening to her go on and on about these happy childhood memories. Living in the moment like they happened only yesterday. I'll never be content and happy like that again. I fucking hate it. That's my new life mantra, I fucking hate. It's all I ever think to myself these days. Frustration builds inside me like a volcano, and the pulsing in my head drowns out her reminiscing.

Sweat builds on my brow and palms, it's too fucking hot in this place. All the little old people on blood thinners, too cold to have the A/C running. I pull at my collar and loosen my tie. I gotta get outta here before I make a scene. I hastily snatch up the photo and shove it in my front pocket, crumpling it. Puzzle pieces scatter from the table all over the floor. I can't stay to help clean up, I gotta get outta this place.

The nurse who comes to help clean up and I collide as I shove my chair back. "Is everything alright over here?" she asks.

"Yeah, she's good, great. She's great." I rub her shoulder and give her a quick peck on the head to soothe her confusion. It's not her fault; there's no way for her to read the change in my mood. I smile at her with what I hope is a warm and encouraging one.

She looks back up at me with unseeing eyes, glassy with confusion and anxiety. She quickly nods her head to the nurse and smiles, trying to seem as though she is still in the moment and knows what's going on. I give her another pat on the back and murmur about seeing her around sometime soon, then jet out of there like my ass is on fire. This is a fucking mess. A whole fucking mess.

FUCK!!!!!! I pound my beer bottle into the wall, smashing it and watching in horror as the glass shards and froth melt down the grimy, painted surface. Yelling into the phone, I curse out Ricky for more than he's worth. "YOU SAID IT WAS A SURE THING!!!" Fuck, fuck, fuck, fuck, fuck this bad, this is so bad. "I'm a dead man," I whisper to myself.

I can't hear what excuse Ricky's yammering on about, can't even register the words, and I don't give a flying fuck anyway. I could've put that $3K toward the gambling debt, but he convinced me I could double it, triple it. How many times has he fucked me over like this? And I keep falling for it over and over again. This'll be the last one cause I'm really a dead man walking right now.

I pace back and forth in front of my beat-up couch, wearing the threadbare carpet of my shit apartment even more. What am I gonna fucking do? What am I fucking gonna do? Ricky keeps talking even though I dropped the phone on the coffee table minutes ago. The angry vibration of a text coming through snaps my attention back to the phone.

It's like a viper waiting to strike me. With trembling hands and bile etching up my throat, I reach for the phone and flip over to see the text that's just come through. Ricky's voice is calling my name, asking if I'm still listening. But I'm frozen, stricken with fear and loathing at what I've read.

> Unknown Number: We'll be seeing you soon.

Chapter 2
The Perfect Find

Willow, three months earlier

MY FEET POUND THE pavement in the early morning quiet. The strikes vibrate up my legs, making my thighs and butt jiggle. Blondie's "Call Me" blares in my ears. My tits swing left and right to the beat; I should have double bra-ed. I'm wheezing, and it feels like someone is twisting a knife between my ribs on my right side.

This last stretch always kicks my ass. Huffing and puffing, I feel like my body is made of lead… maybe my shoes are cement? Maybe I stepped in super gum that is sticking them to the sidewalk? I try to focus on my breathing and concentrate on matching the tempo of the song; the rhythm will help distract me from how tired I feel. Why did I take up jogging? Oh, because I have to have a new hobby every five seconds of my life. I find something to throw myself into for the next three-to-six months, like it's going to be the new me, until I get bored or have a squirrel idea for the next big interest. Oh, God, the side stitches, fuck.

At least I'm doing this in the early morning when the neighborhood is still asleep. No witnesses to my embarrassing flailing down the street. I should have stuck with yoga. Why did I quit yoga? Oh, yeah, I couldn't take the instructor's voice anymore. Too smooth, too soothing. It felt like the class was being led by a late-night radio show host. There should be a yoga class where the instructor talks to you like Samuel L. Jackson.

Can you imagine, *Get your mother fucking ass into mother fucking down dog in the next three mother fucking breaths.* I snort at my own joke and catch my foot on the uneven sidewalk, sending me flying into my neighbor's yard. Argh! My forearm nails the embedded sprinkler head as I go sliding across the grass. That is gonna leave a huge bruise.

Lying in the dewy grass, my lungs heave as I catch my breath. Totally biting it and landing ass up in a stranger's yard is grounds to quit. A little jogging is better than no jogging, *and* I think the universe is telling me that I'm done for today. Who am I to argue with her? I roll to my side and start to stand up just as the sprinklers jerk to life, spraying me down with ice-cold water. Yep, I'm done. I limp the rest of the way home, my ankle and my arm hurting like a bitch.

At least it's not a workday. I get to hang out with my friends and then relax for the evening before hitting the relentless load of my work week. Be a business owner, they said, it'll be fun, they said. Actually, it's pretty amazing, but it is a ton of work. Not today, though; today is a me day. I'm supposed to meet Krista and Jolie for a "treasure hunt" in about an hour, then it's back to Dripping for caffeine and girl time. This should be a good one, too. It's an estate sale in one of the wealthier neighborhoods.

As I continue down the sidewalk, other people's homes start to wake up. Dads are coming out to get the Sunday paper, and people are letting their dogs out... I smile and wave at all my neighbors as

I limp down the sidewalk. I am beat when I finally make it back to my house, and I'm not sure if I even have the energy to climb the steps up to the small craftsman-style home. Trudging up my walkway with slumped shoulders and still holding my side, I wave at my next-door neighbor, Mrs. Graham, as she has her morning cigarette on her porch (still in her bathrobe and curlers). The toe of my shoe catches on the top step, leading to a very ungraceful face plant on my own porch.

I pop up quickly and wave again. "I'm okay!" Not waiting for her to respond, I hustle inside before I do anything else embarrassing. Slamming the door behind me, I promptly trip over the askew doormat, catching myself on the entry table and sending a ba-gillion knick-knacks to the floor. I bend down and gather handfuls of pocket change and the little bowl I keep it and my keys in, and return it all with a plop back on the entry table.

I crawl around on my hands and knees to gather all the little book and movie character figurines and return them to their rightful places. Maybe my mom was right, maybe I have too much stuff. Maybe if I were better at organizing things, my place wouldn't feel so cluttered to her.

I'm a messy person. I try to keep it neat, I really do, but being messy is just natural to me. I think it's because I have to be so meticulous at my coffee shop, you know, health codes and shit, so when I get home, I'm fucking burned out on cleaning up.

She bitches every time she comes to visit about how quaint and cramped my home is. Too small, and there's too much stuff on the walls. Too much stuff on my shelves. *No wonder you can't keep a man, Willow. How does one live with all this junk?*

I like my junk, though; it's special to me, just like my little house. Nothing fancy or extravagant, it's perfectly within my budget and suits my needs.

It's not my junk that runs off any romantic interests. They don't see my junk because it never gets that far. It's because I'm just a little too weird. A little too much of everything. My sense of humor, my taste in music, movies, art... All anyone wants from me are some hot memories they can jack off to in the shower. Show those big jiggly tits and they're happy, ask for anything of depth in return and they run for the hills.

Stop, Willow, you can't go down the pity party vortex right now. I look up toward my ceiling and take a few deep breaths, in and out. No spiraling on me-days. I will not let my mother's vanity ruin my fun day with my friends. A few more calming breaths, and I feel more centered. Time to get ready.

I'm short on time since I walked the rest of my route, but if I multitask, I should be fine. I hustle naked around my kitchen getting the coffee pot going, then back to the bathroom to start the shower warming up and brush my teeth. As I dry off, I walk back to my bedroom, wake up my laptop, and plop down on my bed for one last search for the estate owner. I like getting to know them a little before. It makes buying their belongings more personal. Like I'm building a connection with them, not scavenging their stuff.

It's sad to think about dying, and then people just split all your stuff up like it's nothing. You don't exist anymore, so let's get rid of all your stuff. Belongings that the person loved for whatever reason, the culmination of them making up the person's essence, their life story. It's like having your diary laid out for strangers to rifle through.

I've always believed that if you have an item long enough and love it enough, your energy stays with it. So, if you pass it down, even before you die, some of your essence is shared with the new owner.   I think that's why people have such strong emotional attachments to their belongings. If it were *my* spirit looking down on this, I would feel so exposed, so vulnerable.

Checking my search, I come up empty again. I can't find much of anything about this person online. Oh well, I tried, and now I'm really pushing my time. I don't want to be late.

I throw on some sunscreen and mascara. Hair in a messy bun, check. Eyeliner smudged around my eyes, check. Comfy clothes, check. Gigantic cup of iced coffee with too much sugar, check. I'm out the door and headed to Dripping to meet up with the girls. Careful not to bash into the entry table on my way out, I turn and look back into my sweet little house.

I have this feeling that I'm on the cusp of something big. "Okay, girl, whatever I bring home today, I feel like it's going to be exactly what we were missing." Smiling with the excitement of new beginnings, I walk out the door.

"Woooo sexy bitches!!!!" I holler out of my car window as I pull up to Dripping and see Krista and Jolie already waiting outside. "Ya'll ready to roll?" Krista answers me back with double middle fingers and a "Hell yeah, slut!" She has a loud personality, louder than my own, if you can believe it.

Jolie is the quiet, reserved, friend who balances us out. She just smiles and giggles at Krista's and my antics. I put the SUV in park and the girls jump in, Krista in shotgun and Jolie in the back. She likes it back there 'cause it's quiet compared to being between Krista and me when we get going, trying to outdo each other. Music turned up and really bad singing at the top of our lungs, I put the SUV in gear.

The summer sun is glaring down at us as we unload from my vehicle. Once we are all settled with our haul bags and coffees, we head down the sidewalk. We have to walk about three blocks to get to the actual house. These things draw a crowd, and you have to get here early and wait in line for them to start, or all the good stuff will be gone.

Sometimes, I imagine my life like a movie. If it were, then this would be the opening scene. Krista, Jolie, and me slow-walking down a sidewalk, side by side, to some classic rock song like Ram Jam's Black Betty. Like we are on an important mission or something. Or on our way to kick ass. Or maybe, we accidentally find a real treasure and then bad guys come after us and we have a wild adventure of trying to outrun them...

All dressed in the same style: leggings, band t-shirts, bold jewelry, carrying our shopping bags and coffee mugs. Krista is a little more hardcore with her pink hair and tattoos. She would be our leader, obviously. I could pull a solid sidekick vibe, I think.

Oh my God, I'm already melting. Only 75 degrees today, but it's 87 percent humidity, and I feel like I'm walking into someone else's shower. This is why I went with a black shirt today. I know people think black is hotter to wear in the summer, but I gotta camouflage the sweat marks. My shirt is already sticking to me.

My sunglasses are riding my nose like a Slip N' Slide by the time we get to the address. I shake my ice around and take a big drink of my coffee. Krista turns to me, "So, what did you learn about this person?" She knows my routine of reading the obituary before these things.

My friends lean in to listen as I recount what I found out. "It wasn't very detailed like most others are. Her name was Edith Grant. She was preceded in death by her husband, and she has one son, who, I assume, hired the estate sale company. I know they moved from London to the U.S. during WWII. The only other information it gave was that she *lived a full life.*"

"That's disappointing," Krista says. "They could have said more nice things about her. When I die, you two better write a full-page spread about how amazing I am. I don't care if you have to make shit up."

"We won't have to make up anything, Krista, but we might have to pay to have some things about you expunged." Jolie giggles.

The sale has opened, and the line of people begins to move forward as we are allowed entrance into the property. I pull my gloves out of my bag and slip my iced coffee into the elastic side pocket. Pro-tip: always bring your drink in a spill-proof container that can go in your bag and always, always bring gloves for going through people's long-stored belongings. Never know what kind of critters you might encounter.

The home has a beautiful Tudor-style exterior with red brick and cream trim around the slim windows. Full Indian hawthorn shrubs line the front of the house, with a bed of lantana near the front door. The inside is just as gorgeous. Bold colors and patterns on the walls and furniture. Traditional style chairs and rugs, all marked for sale.

I guess this is a complete sweep. The family doesn't seem to be keeping anything. Poor Edith. Didn't you have anyone in your life who would cherish having some of your belongings to keep? The smell of mothballs and cardboard permeates the air, giving the impression that this house hasn't been really lived in for a while.

A haunting feeling of lost hope and forgotten dreams pulses through my veins like ice water. I follow Krista and Jolie through the property, determined to do my part to remember Edith. Giving new purpose to others' possessions makes me feel connected to the universe, like your spirit can transcend time and space even after you've passed on. Maybe Edith didn't have family interested in keeping her memory alive, but I can show her spirit respect by cherishing something of hers for the future.

We stop in one of the back bedrooms that has been filled with cardboard boxes that look like they haven't seen the outside of an attic for a long time. Gloved and ready to search, we each take a different box. The girls and I have done this so many times that we are pretty good at spying what one of the others would be interested in, so we have taken a 'divide and conquer' approach to hunting at the big sales like this one.

There are old British newspapers from the 1940s wrapped around fragile items. It makes me think that Edith packed these items when she and her husband left London back then, never to be opened again.

The boxes are filled with a crazy variety of stuff: African pottery, candles (all of which are melted and misshapen), a taxidermized squirrel, and uhhhhhh, is this someone's teeth on a necklace? Gross.

Most of the fragile items have been broken or damaged some-how. I wonder if whoever brought them out for the sale mishan-dled them. Again, I'm hit with sadness for Edith and the lack of care anyone seems to have for her after her passing. I'm lost in those thoughts while digging to the bottom of my box when I strike gold! Okay, not literal gold, but it's something very, very cool.

It's a statue that looks about one foot tall. I wipe away some dust and newspaper shreds to see the vivid red color and what looks like a man in a red cloak seated on a stool with his hands in his pockets. He has a mischievous expression, like he knows a juicy secret.

I feel an instant connection to this piece, as if it wanted me to find it. I'm lost in a trance-like stare at the little statue's crinkled ceramic face when Krista pokes me in the ribs. "Look how cool that is! He will look perfect on your bookshelf at home."

I slowly break my gaze away from his face and turn my treasure around for my friends to see. Jolie leans in for a closer look. "Willow, I think your statue is actually a bottle." She reaches over and wiggles the hat, revealing a cork attached.

The statue is mounted on some kind of stone base, it's roughly cut and porous. Turning the bottle back and forth, I find a small engraving of entwined hearts, a maker's mark possibly? Another strange symbol of interconnected lines is carved into the bottom; it doesn't look like letters or numbers. I run my thumb over it and then quickly pull my hand back, shocked at how scorching hot it is. I tentatively try again, only this time it's cool to the touch.

"I wonder what it's like on the inside." I ponder, half to myself. Krista leans closer, "I don't think you should open it. What if the cork is rotted and breaks?" We all look closer at the top of the statue. Jolie playfully elbows me and says, "Even if it isn't rotten, you might unleash some kind of ghosty that's been trapped inside. That's right up your alley, Willow." I giggle at her as I move to place the statue in my bag to purchase on the way out. "You know," I smile, "that might be exciting."

I unlock the back door of Dripping, then take my bag back from Krista. We file inside, and I hit the lights as we go. It was a good day, but I feel whooped, probably from all the humidity. "Okay, ladies, the usuals?" I head behind the counter, fire up the espresso machine, and start getting out snacks. My friends nod and slump into our favorite booth for our private coffee dates. They are whooped, too. Caffeine: We all need caffeine.

While I wait for the espresso to drip, I open my canvas bag and rummage around for my statue. I pull him free and unwrap the butcher paper that's crumpled around him. Hmm... scanning the coffee shop, I search for a nice place to put him. Better to go ahead and place him somewhere than for him to get broken.

Ah ha! There's a shelf next to the main entrance that needs something with a little height to make the existing arrangement more interesting. I adjust him to the perfect angle among the displayed books and a little bud vase. His red color fits in perfectly with the shop's motif. He needs a name. I stare at him for a bit with my finger on my chin, "Humphrey, I'll call you Humphrey, don't ask me why."

When I eventually get the coffee and snacks out to the girls, I want to melt into the booth cushion. I take a big swig from my Jaws mug, then lay the questions on Jolie about her date the other day. She came in with this dick head from up the street. He owns the sporting goods store, and there are rumors that he is trying to buy up the block.

I know Jolie is trying not to lose it over the news. She worked so hard starting over with her life after her terrible ex-husband drama. Her shop is her life, her creative outlet; losing it would be devastating for her.

I'm probably low on the chopping block if Scott is really trying to obtain all the property. Although the aesthetic probably doesn't resonate with his clientele. I look around my little slice of business heaven and try to imagine a bunch of middle-aged men in hunter's orange and athleisure hanging out in my gothic coffee house.

Jim Bob could order a "Willy's Wonka" with an "O ring with Cream" on the side (a mocha latte with whip cream, cookie stick and chocolate shavings and a plain bagel with cream cheese... yeah people don't bring their kids here) and have a seat in the red crushed velvet booth while enjoying the musical stylings of Mareux.

I giggle into my coffee cup at the thought. But if he does buy the block, I would probably lose a significant amount of customer volume. Honestly, his buying Book Ends and Love Your Skin will be enough to put a dent in all of our businesses. This place works as a community; we need each other.

After we finish our lunch, Krista and Jolie head down the block to her shop to drop off their goodies, and I get started prepping for tomorrow. I can get fresh fruit prepped for my little charcuteries I serve and mix my dry ingredients for my muffins, so the morning goes a little smoother.

I talk to the shop as I work. I developed a habit of talking to my coffee shop like she is one of my best friends. I heard someone say that you should treat places that are emotionally connected to you as if they have their own spirit, ever since I started talking to my house and my coffee shop.

The faucet is running, and I'm elbow-deep in suds when the lights flicker. Frozen for only a second, I reach out to the dry mat for the knife I used earlier on the fruit. I'm not usually spooked being here on my own, but with all this talk of Scott being up to no good and the eerie quiet of the empty café, it puts me a little on edge.

Nothing happens for a moment, and then the lights flicker again. Just the one over my head where I stand at the sink. The electric buzzing and pale blue hue of the bulb going in and out. Then the one by the main entrance.

My wall sconces seem to get brighter for a moment. What the fuck is going on? The lights dance like this, taking turns glowing brighter and dimmer, and my heart pounds in my chest. "Stop!" I yell into the empty café like a crazy person. But it works.

Everything goes back to normal. I white knuckle the knife as the hairs on my arms rise. I get the feeling I'm being watched. With measured steps and my brandished sword, I walk the main seating area and check under booths and tables for anything suspicious. Pulling on the main entrance door, I double-check all the locks and reassure myself nobody is here with me.

"Dripping, you bitch." Still feeling adequately freaked out, I finish cleaning up and get packed to go. I lock up and take one more look around. Everything seems legit. I hit the lights and set the alarm. "See you tomorrow, girl."

Chapter 3
One Stormy Night

Willow, current

THE THUNDER STARTED ON my way home from Dripping. Deep and boisterous, announcing the arrival of doom from above. The weather station kept predicting an epic rain event, but each day, they would push it back. I was beginning to think it wasn't going to happen. The humidity was so thick these past few days, though, it's overdue for rain.

I turn the radio dial to the 24-hour weather station as I make my way down the street. The announcer is wired with excitement for the potential threat from this system. The station crackles in and out, and the thunder outside is getting louder and closer together. *One Mississippi, two Mississippi, three Mississippi, four Mississippi*— BOOM!

The thunder is so loud that I jump in my car seat and yank the steering wheel slightly. It's followed by an angry flash of lightning. The radio station crackles, the sound of the meteorologist coming back into range— *Wow, folks, this system is a real beast. We are going to have heavy wind and rain over the next 48 hours, potentially.*

Fayetteville can expect to be under a tornado watch tonight and through tomorrow. The city department of transportation is advis-

ing that all non-essential traffic stay off the roadways. Please, folks, for your safety and the safety and ease of first responders who may be needed at this time, please stay home, hunker down.

I turn my car around and head back to Dripping. If this storm is going to be such a doozy, then I need to put a sign on the coffee shop. Heavy drops of rain are already starting to hammer at my windshield. I don't have any rain gear in my car, so I pull up as closely as I can to the back and make a run for the door. My keys slip around in my hand as I try to find the small black bat-shaped key to fit the lock. I'm soaked once I finally get the door open.

I slip off my shoes by the entrance and rush into my office to snatch a sheet of printer paper, a marker, and tape. Trying not to drip water all over the page, I quickly write, *Closed due to Inclement Weather.* I slip on the wet linoleum— I'm dripping little puddles everywhere— so I grab two hand towels from the kitchen and ride them like skis over to the front door to tape up my sign.

The bang of the back door being blown back and forth by the wind startles me. Shit, I didn't shut it when I rushed in, and the rain is blowing inside. I can hear it pelting on the floor. I'm making a huge mess in my effort to be expeditious. As I tape all four corners of my sign to the front door, lightning strikes again.

It's so bright I'm temporarily blinded, and the thunderclap that accompanies it vibrates the walls of the coffee shop, making all my decorations rattle. The shadowy outline of a person flashes against the glass of the front door for a brief second. Before I can make sense of it, Humphrey tips over the edge of the shelf; I catch him just in time to prevent him from shattering on the floor. Another strike of lightning bursts through the clouds. I tuck him under my arm and ski back toward the office.

A small lake has accumulated near the back entrance, seeping toward my office and the back storage room entrance. I sweep my feet around in my helter-skelter attempt to mop up as much as I can with the towels I'm standing on.

The door continues to dance back and forth in the wind until it swings forward with a violent bang. The wind is howling; I need to get home quickly before it gets any more dangerous to be on the road.

Leaving the towels spread out on the linoleum, I scoop up my shoes, not even bothering to put them on, and race to my car. The wind is so strong that I have to forcefully slam my driver's door closed. It's then that I realize I never put Humphrey down. He's still squished in my armpit. My shoes thump on the floorboard of the front passenger side, and I click the seatbelt around him. Guess he's coming home with me.

My SUV hums to life, and the wipers flap so hard against the rain they might fly off the windshield. Visibility is shit. I creep along the highway, following what I hope is a safe distance behind the taillights of the poor soul driving in front of me. Buddy, if you take a ditch, I'm right behind you.

The frenzied rhythm of my wiper blades pushes my storm anxiety through the roof. The vehicle in front of me stops short, and I crank the wheel to the right to keep from rear-ending it and swerve toward the ditch. The seatbelt locks up across my chest, and I reflexively stretch a protective arm out for Humphrey, but the seatbelt holds him tight.

A large tree branch has fallen and is blocking most of the lane. I follow the other vehicle slowly over the shoulder of the road, my

SUV barely keeping my right tires on the edge before the drop off of the ditch.

I'm so thankful to finally be pulling up in my driveway. The rain splashes around my tires as I turn over the curb into my carport. I cut the engine and dash into the house. The rain was coming down so hard that between running in and out of the coffee shop, my clothes are completely soaked. I feel like I jumped into a lake.

Tip-toeing through my kitchen and hallway as quickly as I can, stripping off my heavy, wet clothing as I go, and then chucking it straight into the washing machine that sits across the hall from the bathroom. Even my brain is chattering from the cold, and I can't wait to boil myself under the hot water.

Steam fills the small bathroom from the shower, so thick I can barely see past an arm's reach. I bend down to shut off the faucet and release the diverter. Goosebumps rise on my arms despite how hot and steamy the bathroom has gotten. Something out of place flashes in my peripheral. I whip upright and peer through the curtain at the dark shadow that's shaped like a man.

My heart is pounding in my throat. I hold perfectly still; I don't move, and neither does he. My mind races, trying to simultaneously problem-solve the likelihood someone could be in my home— *did I lock the door when I ran inside*— and what I can do to defend myself. Without breaking the direction of my gaze, I reach up and fumble for the detachable showerhead. At least I could use that to beat at the intruder.

Focusing on slowing my breaths, I grip the opposite end of the shower curtain and rip it open, ready to strike— at nothing. There's nothing here, no one. My chest hurts from the bashing of my heart against my ribs. What could have caused the shadow? I pull the curtain back and forth, trying to see the shadow again, but I can't recreate it.

The steam slowly dissipates as the bathroom cools off. I stand in the tub shivering, still holding the showerhead. I know what I saw...

The towel I pulled from the cabinet earlier is hung neatly on the hook right next to the shower. I know I left it folded on the vanity. I know I did. There's no one in the bathroom with me. The door is closed, and the lock is still flipped. I always lock the door even though I live alone.

Wrapping the towel around myself, I put my ear to the bathroom door and hold my breath, listening for any movement on the other side. Okay, Willow, think logically. If there was a man standing in the bathroom with me, he couldn't have gotten out the door so quickly without you hearing it.

I didn't bring any clothes in here with me, so I'm stuck naked in this towel if I open the door and there's a murderer! Holy shit, what am I gonna do? The doorknob looks like a traitor right now. The lock button is clearly turned, but I try the knob slowly anyway, and it doesn't budge. I jerk a little harder just to be sure, and it holds tight. Rationally, I know there probably wasn't anyone in the bathroom just now. I saw the shadow until I pulled the curtain; I would have seen it move if the person went out the bathroom door.

Taking the hairspray can from my vanity, I pop the lid and place my index finger on the top, ready to spray at the first sign of a threat. This is the next best thing to pepper spray. I make sure my towel is secure, slowly turn the lock, and rip the door open as fast as I can.

"Take that fucker!" I crop dust my hallway with anti-humidity extra hold, but nothing. Stalking around my little house, I check closets, under my bed, and behind doors... my doors and windows are all locked and secure. I guess I really just freaked myself out over nothing.

The storm continues to roar outside, thunder and lightning punctuating the night sky. The force of the wind shakes my windows now and then. I change into comfy lounge pants and make my last pack of noodles in the microwave. I really need to go to the grocery store.

I pace the kitchen while the microwave runs and pull up the Instagram account for Dripping. Making a little reel about the coffee shop being closed tomorrow due to Storm-pocalypse, the microwave beeps just as I finish up posting. It sucks that this storm is so serious, but I'm not going to complain about a day off to cozy on the couch and listen to the rain while I read. This calls for hot chocolate. I grab a mug, a hot cocoa packet, and turn to the cabinet for a spoon.

My kitchen utensil drawer always sticks; a few jerks, and it comes bursting free, sending utensils flying out. I bend down to pick them up from the kitchen floor. Out of the corner of my eye, I catch something shadowy in the reflection of the stove door. The terror I felt in the bathroom earlier surges upward from my gut to my throat. Gripping a fork in my right hand, I slowly stand up, ready to stab a fucker. But there's nobody there, again. What the fuck am I seeing? At this point, I almost wish there was an intruder so I wouldn't think I was losing my marbles.

The backdrop of this crazy storm outside must have my mind going to creepy places. I admonish myself for getting riled up again while I throw the fork back into the drawer and fish out my Hello Kitty chopsticks and a spoon for the hot chocolate. I take my noodles and mug to the couch and tuck my legs under a blanket. Slurping noodles while I surf the streaming services for something good to watch. An alert on my weather app flashes at me about wind speeds and rain levels.

I'm just about to hit select on a murder mystery I've been waiting to watch when the lights go out. All the subtle noises of my home I take for granted, lulls to nothing. The A/C unit shuts down, and my fan slowly loses momentum. The only light is the glow from my cell phone and the occasional flash of lightning.

There goes movie night. My cellphone flashlight illuminates my feet as I pad back to the kitchen and place my bowl in the sink, then head to the bathroom to brush my teeth by cellphone light. I climb into bed and listen to the rain while lying there in silence. Thoughts of the shadow I saw through the shower curtain running through my mind.

Living alone is super glamorous, you get to decorate how you want, eat what you want, come and go as you please... have total control of the TV... Until something creepy happens, and then you get to be scared all by yourself, too. It looked so real. Like a man standing there watching me wash all my best bits.

I like spooky stories, dark romance, and vintage horror. Have I finally rotted my brain with all of these that I'm hallucinating? I can't shake the feeling that I wasn't alone when I was naked and distracted in the shower. I'm starting to wonder if I need to see a professional. I have been hallucinating like this a lot in the last few months. The feeling that I'm not alone, that someone's hand is on my shoulder or my face, glimpses of someone just outside of my peripheral...

Then there have been the weird lighting issues at Dripping... and I swear sometimes I hear a man's voice. I tried talking to Krista about all the weird stuff, but she just joked that maybe I'm being haunted by a ghost with a crush and said, "Let's hope he's hot."

The intensity of the rain grows outside my window. Lightning flashes from behind my curtains like a strobe light escaping from the edges of the material. I roll to my back and stare up at the darkness.

It tracks for me that the only man I could get to be interested is a ghost of my own hallucinogenic conjuring. My insecurities come rushing in; I'm too weird, too spooky, not spooky enough, too independent... The parade of failed relationship experiments dances through my mind.

My need to have a new hobby for creative expression made me seem flighty and inconsistent. My spooky vibes were too fringe or not fringe enough, so then I was a poser. And don't get me started on being a girl boss. I wasn't available often enough for them, or they were intimidated by my drive.

My eyelids flutter as I start to feel drowsy, soothed by the rhythm of rain on my windowsill despite the violence of the thunder and lightning, as I slip deeper. I'm not sure how long I've been asleep, when I'm roused by the sensation of my blanket being pulled from my body. Warmth turns to chills at the change as the draft of the rainy fall night breezes over my skin.

Groggily, I reach my hand over the bed, trying to find the blanket's edge to cover back up, but it eludes me. A different warmth covers my skin; in my half-sleep state, I'm not alarmed by the comforting weight ghosting over my body.

Caught somewhere between dreaming and waking, I imagine feather-light caresses trail over my breast, then down my stomach to between my legs. I run my hands over myself, chasing after the path, but nothing is there; my hands move unhindered over my lounge clothes. The sensation teases me, still sleepy and not motivated to rouse more; my legs graze across my cotton sheets, bending and spreading. I run my hand over my clothed pussy, matching the sensation I'm dreaming about.

The pressure over my center is just enough to register. I slip my hand under my waistband, through wet, smooth skin, until I make contact with my clit with a content sigh. The feeling of being touched, breathed on, and licked has me circling my clit and undulating my hips in time with the sensations. I'm more awake now. The thunder has subsided, and soft rain patters against the window.

My bedroom is a soft glow from the moon seeping through the cracks in my curtains. My head lolls to the side as I ride my fingers, the orgasm building. So very close to the edge. My breath quickens just as I'm about to cross that precipice into climactic pleasure... I see him, my shadow, at the foot of my bed... I jolt upright, and instead of calling out my orgasm, I scream in absolute terror— a loud pop— and all my lights come back on. There's nothing there.

"Welcome to Dripping for Your Pleasure," I call out into the coffee shop as I hear the door chime. I finish washing up the pitcher from the iced coffee I just made before I turn to greet my new guest. "What are we thinking?" I turn around with a warm smile plastered on my face. The man at my counter, however...

He looks gruff, ragged. His eyes are hollow and dark, like he hasn't slept much in a long time, and he smells strongly of cigarettes. There's a deep scar on his left cheekbone just underneath his eye; whatever gave him that must have really hurt.

He hasn't spoken yet and doesn't appear to be looking at the menu. Instead, he is looking all around my shop. I get it; the decorations here can be unsettling if you aren't a kindred spooky soul.

"Can I get you a coffee or something to eat?" I try again to regain his attention. He distractedly orders a plain black coffee, his voice just as coarse as you would have expected. He lays a few dollars on the counter absently as he turns away from me, too invested in the shop décor to be any more social.

I pour his coffee and lay his change back on the counter next to the to-go cup. He's looking from wall to wall around the shop. "Are you a fan of classic horror?" I ask.

"What? Huh?" he turns back toward the counter.

"I asked if you like classic horror. You know, like Dracula or Creature from the Black Lagoon?" I nod my head toward the old movie posters hanging on the wall.

"Oh, no, not really. I'm more into antiques." He picks up the change and shoves it roughly into his pocket.

"Oh, I love thrifting! If you are looking for unique stuff, you should try my friend's shop up the block, Jolie's Eclectic and Vinyl."

He nods his head while he studies my face. I feel unnerved suddenly. Maybe I shouldn't have recommended Jolie's store. He takes one more look around at my decorations and walks out of the coffee shop. "Oh, hey, you forgot your coffee— " I call after him, but he doesn't turn around.

Chapter 4

Willow

"What is existence?" I ask. Lying across an old dusty trunk, I turn my head toward Philip, waiting for a reply. He never does when I ask these questions, just blinks back at me with his tiny black sage eyes, waiting for me to find my own answers. I've been in the midst of an existential crisis for the last several decades with no end in sight. Perhaps my fate is to be tortured by philosophical pondering for eternity.

Lurking in the attic seems befitting. Now that the house is unoccupied, where else should a man doomed to skulk in the shadows for eternity take up? I am resigned to spending my eternal days bearing witness to the decay of everything around me while I remain. Philip scampers over to a hollowed-out space in the beam where he's been stashing nuts, and he looks over his shoulder suspiciously in my direction. "I told you *already*, I didn't take any of your nuts." Rolling my eyes in exasperation, I turn my gaze back to the attic ceiling and continue my endless pondering of my purpose and the inner workings of the universe.

As usual, I come up empty-handed.

Every time I found something that sparked hope, no result. Scouring Edith's extensive collection of books on the occult, desperately looking for clues on how to pass on to the other side, has proved fruitless. This attic is littered with failed attempts at candles, herbs, and sigils drawn in the dust on the floor, scratched into the wooden planks... cleansing spells... Apparently, you can't banish yourself. I feel exhausted. Still, I force myself to continue; it's only been a few decades after all. It hardly seems respectable to give up hope after such a short period, when you have the endless road of time to walk?

Something tickles behind my neck; a wash of trepidation coats my insides as the tickle travels closer to the edge of my collar, and I shoot off the trunk onto the attic floor with a clunk. Spiders, ugh!! "Philip! Why didn't you warn me?!" He squeaks at me and scampers off out of the little hole in the attic window while I convulse like I've been electrocuted.

Sunlight teases at the windowsill where he vanished. A taunt of all the things I took for granted. I stare out after Philip, ever envious of his ability to come and go as he pleases, unlike me. I miss the feel of the sun on my skin on a long walk. The freedom to choose whether I stay or go. The intimate touch of another person...

Movement in front of the house catches my eye. The sound of car doors shutting and voices drift up to the attic window, curious. Making my way downstairs, I'm just passing through the living room when I hear the turn of the lock on the front door, *Gerald*. I'm surprised to see him back here so soon, but he isn't alone. This time, he is followed by a crew of people. He immediately starts giving a tour of the home and pointing out all of the furnishings and drapes.

This is really happening, then. It's what I expected, sure, but I had tried to turn my mind from the reality. Edith is gone, and now everything is going to change. Now, I will be *truly* forgotten. Attached to the vicinity of the bottle, once it's tossed or locked in storage, that will be the end of any semblance of life for me and any chance I had to find peace.

I feel sick watching the masses file into Edith's home, fighting over her belongings. I fidget with the ring in my pocket, twisting it around the tip of my index finger as the old biddies fight over drapes and teacups. The house once held vibrance and the eclectic magic of a life well-lived. Gerald reduced it to a meat market. He's such a selfish fucking prick. He never appreciated his mother, only what she could give him. Always coming around to beg off for money. Lifting pieces of the fine silver and then telling Edith she must have misplaced it. Using her failing mind against her to mask his betrayal. Scavenging off her most treasured life possessions as if they were rotting carrion. Opportunistic fuck.

The kitchen is in complete disarray; the contents of every cabinet have been emptied and placed on display. Edith would have a fit over the state of it. I can picture Edith sitting at the kitchen counter, sipping her tea from that cup, it was her favorite. Its dainty blue and pink floral pattern on the cup and matching saucer reminded her of her home back in England. The hag currently tucking it between her arm and her giant, saggy titty doesn't deserve to enjoy it. "Does the tea bags inside the canister come with it? 'Cause I ain't paying extra for those," she screeches.

Before she can get an answer and before I can get a rational thought, I smack the tea tin right out of old saggy titties' hands. Her offended expression turns icy with fear as the primal part of her brain begins to register that something isn't quite right in this house. Gently taking the teacup and returning it to its rightful place next to the kettle, I prepare to uncork the rage and hurt brewing inside of me. Sick of sitting on the sidelines while Edith's memory is dashed to rubbish, my anger pushes my energy to the cusp of volcanic chaos. Saggy titties' hair starts to blow back from her forehead, and she squints into the force of wind coming directly at only her. I'm seconds away from pulling some serious poltergeist shit to scare all of these people out of the house—

Creamy vanilla scent fills my nose, soothing my anger, followed by the sound of a sweet voice. I turn away from the saggy titty hag and head past the kitchen's doorway, obligated to the pursuit of that smell. I can see the entry hall leading to the front door. Her face haloed in the soft light filtering through the living room windows— I am knocked cold from my grief and hatred, slingshot straight into obsession. Blind to the scavengers still casting their lots around me. I am enamored.

As if tethered by invisible bonds, I trail behind her as she explores the house. Her creamy vanilla scent calms my energy, beckoning me to get closer. Inhaling deeply, I anchor myself to this moment. Her expression of reverence as she navigates the home, like she is trying to envision the life that once thrived here, soothes the angry cracks of my heart.

She stops in Edith's old sewing room, now filled with the contents of the attic. The boxes had been tossed carelessly into the center of the room, with the vultures tearing through them. All the little oddities Edith loved so much... including my bottle.

These boxes had previously been ravaged by Gerald behind Edith's back as he searched in vain for some secret treasure. The value here was always the love Edith felt for them, not money. They represented the life her parents led, their adventures. They were tangible connections to their tales of travel. I remember the tender way Edith packed every box as she and her husband prepared to flee the war.

I walked next to my vanilla siren, whispering in her ear, coaxing her toward a very important cardboard box sitting on the floor. My body tingles with anticipation as I lean in, brushing my fingertips along her jawline, stealing a touch, as I lift her hair away from her ear. Whispering, pleading to her, *please, please, please,* I beg with everything in my being. *Find my bottle; take me home.*

Current

The smell of coffee is invigorating. I loved coffee when I was alive; I could have guzzled it by the potful if I were able. Inhaling deeply and holding it in, I attempt to stain my nostrils with the scent. It's infused in Willow's home too. Even her skin seems to be varnished in the fragrance, coffee and cream. I half expected her pussy to taste like a cupcake. Creamy, yes, very creamy, but a delicious, tangy flavor, to be both savored and devoured.

Being left behind in the coffee shop, I'm tortured by the smell. The consuming aroma triggering memories of some delightfully dirty times we've had together. I smile at the thoughts as I wander around. This place's kitchen is impressive for a small space. Metal countertops and large machines for making elaborate coffees line either side of the galley-style space. Stores of fruits and bread in containers. I miss eating. I can still taste and smell and all that, but there isn't a need to eat now. No hunger to drive me, unless it's Willow's pussy, of course. Sleep is the same way. I don't need to sleep; I can sleep, but the satisfaction of resting to relieve exhaustion is gone. I mostly do it because I get bored.

I meander toward the main seating area. This place reminds me of Edith's shop. Cushy velvet chairs, bold red colors, ghastly decorations. I pause in front of— I think this is a human skull that's been encrusted with... black crystals? And an iron wall sconce of a bat, he is hanging upside down with a small lightbulb cradled in each of his wings. I look upward as I start to sit at one of the little bistro tables and shoot right out of the chair, *what the fuck*! Right above me, dangling from the ceiling, is a dangling, giant spider with huge fangs and glowing eyes. How have I not noticed that until now? I fucking hate spiders... even fake ones.

I flop myself down in one of the plush booths instead and blow a little whiff over a napkin that's sticking up from the dispenser. This is what I've become. A ghost spending his eternity practicing parlor tricks to pass the time. Being in Willow's presence makes me feel as though I have purpose again. Without her, though, I'm fucking bored. I've been brainstorming ways to get her attention again. Moving items in the kitchen... I wrote her name in whipped cream on the countertop, but it all melted into a single puddle before she saw it.

I've tried repeating my little light show in the evenings. But that one doesn't go over very well. I really wasn't trying to scare her, but I only have so many tricks. General poltergeist abilities. Flashing lights, moving things about short distances, slamming doors, things like that. Interestingly, the only object I've never been able to move is the bottle. That little fucker.

That stormy night when I had the accidental fortune of riding home with Willow was a nexus experience. Now, she brings me home with her any time there is a threat of bad weather. I can't take my eyes off her, I can't separate myself from her for even a moment when she is near. Curiously, she seems to feel my presence now and then. That's new. Not even Edith, with all her attempts to engage with me, ever seemed to be able to physically sense me. This gives me some hope, but hope can be a dangerous thing.

I used to spend my days angry, reflecting on why I was so stupid on that fateful day. Angry and jealous of Isabelle and her privileged life, getting to move forward, grow old, and experience the liberty that is death. To have an end to your existence is a luxury the living take for granted.

I was a bloody idiot that day, for sure. All I can say is that I was not thinking clearly. I wonder what Isabelle did with her life. Did she marry that bastard? Live happily ever after? Probably never gave me a second thought, never wondered why I vanished off the face of the earth.

No one did. There wasn't anyone who would. I had no family. Maybe Jack? My best friend. My only friend, really. He knew I was planning to ask Isabelle to marry me that day, tried to warn me off her. Maybe he looked for me. I try not to dwell too much on it these days. Nothing can be done anyway, so what's the point? I stretch my arms back over the top of the booth seat and tip my head to the ceiling. Closing my eyes to the past. Everyone I have ever known is dead now. That is a lonelier feeling than the idea of existing forever.

Edith treated me as if I still possessed some degree of person-hood. She kept my bottle on the bookshelf in the living room. Her family found the bottle and her attachment to it unnerving, especially Gerald; I suppose I can understand that. Especially when your very eccentric mother talks to a little statue when she thinks no one is looking. I think she had her suspicions about what hap-pened to me that day. After she passed, the bottle was one of the first of her belongings to get packed away. Gerald couldn't get rid of it fast enough. I'm lucky he didn't chuck it straight away into the rubbish bin. Then I'd be stuck haunting a landfill for the rest of eternity.

It's still night outside, the moon shining through the glass win-dows. I'm sprawled out on one of the benches "sleeping," well, actually, I'm reliving this one night in her bedroom, teasing her sweet pussy, when I'm disturbed by a rattling sound coming from the back of the café.

Jumping up from my lounge, I head to the back and pass through to the other side to find Willow fighting with her keys to unlock the door. She is loaded down with a large purse, a backpack, and two large drink containers. Her hair is falling in her face, and she can't see the keyhole, so she is stabbing blindly at the door. I reach out with my hand to lift her blonde blindfold so she can finally get the key seated in the lock.

"Fucking finally." She mutters. I crack a smile and say, "I'm so sorry, my love, I would have come sooner if you had only called my name." I know she can't hear me, but it feels human to talk back to her. And I like her sassy mouth. Damn it all, now I can't look away from her mouth. Her juicy lips, painted a sparkly red. They glitter enticingly like a shiny ripe apple, tasty and ready to bite... I imagine licking the seam of them like I've licked the seam of her pussy. How her pussy wept for me while she lay there dreaming, a sticky little puddle dripping onto her bedsheet. Could I make her mouth drool like too? So enraptured in pleasure that she dripped for me from both places?

Willow waddles inside with her belongings and dumps them in a small office just off the kitchen. She makes her way through the back of the café, turning on lights in the office, the back storage room, and the kitchen area. She returns and makes herself a fancy espresso drink, filled to the brim with froth and cream; she even opted to adorn it with little sprinkles, adorable.

She takes her dessert in a cup with her as she walks to the other side of the café, with me following along close behind her. I suppose this will be my new normal, following Willow around. I have zero complaints. She lovingly plucks the bottle from the shelf and carries him over to one of the little bistro tables.

Taking a seat, she sets down the oversized coffee mug, pops the lid on a container of cleaning wipes, and pulls a sheet free. Bracing the bottle on the tabletop, she wipes methodically, getting all the nooks and crannies where dirt and dust from the years have settled. I can't help myself; taking a seat on the tabletop, I spread my thighs, so the statue juts from between my legs. Licking my lips, I grin absurdly as she continues her ministrations. Pumping and twisting her hand around the statue between my legs has me salivating.

She giggles, and I feel it in my balls. "I know we've only just met, but excuse me, Humphrey, while I give you a proper bath." Hmm, the imagery of lying in a tub with Willow, covered in soapy water while she rubs my body down with a cloth. Imagining her wrapping her soap-slicked palm around my hard cock while I wash her bountiful breasts and pinch her nipples...

Now I've got a raging hard cock from dreaming of being naked with Willow. I slip my hand into my trousers and free myself, stroking in time with her to match how she's polishing my bottle. Bless her for being so thorough, too. She wipes gently with her thumb around the head of the bottle, and I mirror her circular motion with my thumb around the head of my cock, gripping and squeezing down my shaft as she works down the body of the bottle. I cum with a groan, catching my mess in my hand.

Willow looks around the café as if she's heard something, her sweet mouth pops open in confusion. Before I've even thought it through, I lean forward, reaching out and brushing my cum-soaked thumb over her bottom lip. Her hand shoots up to touch her mouth, then her tongue swipes along her lush, red skin.

Standing in front of her with my still-hard cock bobbing level with her face, I continue to stroke myself as she licks her lips a second time, crinkling her eyebrows as she tries to discern the taste. Interesting, I wasn't expecting that she would feel me touch her, let alone taste a hint of my cum on her lips.

Sweet Willow, so innocently perched before me. No idea that my hard, pulsing, cock is a mere breath from her mouth, aching to spill a second time all over her face, neck, and breasts. The innocent expression of confused intrigue has my cock pulsing. I imagine rubbing my cum into her skin, massaging the thick splashes into her breasts... into her clit... stuffing it into her pussy with my fingers... I pump my shaft. I can't stop, my orgasm barreling down on me like a freight train as I lose myself in the siren sitting in front of me.

Just as I crest the edge a second time, Willow stands from the chair and moves to put away the cleaning wipes. With her back turned to me, I pivot my hips and release myself into her coffee mug, gasping and grunting out my climax. The thick ropes of cum plop into the caffeinated concoction with little splashes and drips over the rim.

When she returns for the cup, I watch with rapt attention to see if she'll taste me. My heart hammers in anticipation as she lifts it to her lips. She takes a deep pull of her creamed coffee. The warmth that spreads in my chest knowing she's drinking my cum. Her eyebrows draw together at the new flavor, and she pulls her face away with a little whipped topping coating her lips. Watching her tongue glide along them as she cleans herself up has me groaning and aching to reach for my cock again. She looks back at the cup, at first offended, but then she swallows again, savoring the new flavor. She smiles and continues to drink. Perfect girl. If only I could taste your lips afterward.

Her ass sways deliciously as she moves to the chalkboard menu, where she writes her daily specials. Willow stands in contemplation with one hand on her hip and the other under her chin, with her index finger over her soft lips. Soft, plump lips, lips I could suck on while her pussy soaks my aching cock. My thoughts are all in the bloody gutter when she's near. Fuck, I'm a bastard for this. But I'm not sorry. I hop onto the counter, so I can face her and relish her beauty. Mind settled, she raises her chalk and in artful script, she adds to the board: Today's special: *The Humphrey Bag-Art: Horseradish, Gruyere, and Prosciutto on a toasted Onion Bagel.*

"There you go, Humphrey, your own menu item." She dusts the chalk from her hands and goes back to the sink to rewash. Humphrey, she's called me that name since the first day. Willow doesn't even know me, and she's already given me a sweet pet name and a sandwich. I think I'm in love.

Late afternoon descends, and the café traffic winds down. The evening rush now finished, Willow prepares for closing soon. It's half six on the clock, her door sign shows she closes at seven p.m. during the weekdays. Long hours for her to be here by herself. It was half five this morning when she came in to prepare for the opening. There's a lull in the day when she has breaks, and she closes for about two hours in the afternoon when business isn't steady, but there's no way that is enough rest.

I've enjoyed spending time with her. She is kind and chatty with the customers, and her ass wiggles delectably as she scrubs down the kitchen. I'm just about to wrap my arms around her waist and take a deep inhale of her coffee-cream scent from her neck when the door chimes.

A last-minute customer, perhaps? I follow Willow to the door to greet a very disgusting man in faded and stained dungarees. There are sweat stains under his arms and around his neck where patchy chest hair peaks out. He doesn't look as if he's seen a bar of soap in months and smells of it, too. The front of his tool kit reads *Arnie's Electric*. Shit. I suppose my little light shows have caused her to think she needs her wiring checked. Fuck me, I've messed up.

"Hi, are you Arnie? The electrician?" Willow hesitates to hold out her hand for a shake, wisely apprehensive at his unkept appearance. He aggressively takes her hand in his and squeezes a little at her wrist. The bastard. His smug reply, "Says so on the toolbox, darling."

He gives her a sleezy half-toothed grin as he lifts the box upward to show off his business logo. Is this really the best the city has to offer in the way of an electrician? She steps aside cautiously from the threshold, reluctantly allowing him entrance, and I place myself between them. He isn't getting closer to my Willow.

Bumbling in a waddly gait, he walks himself back toward the kitchen with Willow hurrying to head him off. "Oh, wait, if you're looking for the primary fuse box, that will be in the storage room back this way." She opens her arms wide to block him from entering the kitchen. I don't blame her; that would be a sanitation nightmare.

He leans in a little too close to brush his arm over her breast as he turns and heads toward the storage closet. What the fuck? I need to do something, or this pig of a man will continue trying to steal little touches. I follow behind him to the storage closet, contemplating murder.

I could make a heavy box fall on his head. I could turn over a flavored syrup bottle, so he slips and hits his head on the floor. The image of him lying in the closet, limp and bleeding out, brings a smile to my face, but then I'm quickly ashamed of myself; my poor Willow would bear the burden of blame in that scenario, and I can't have that. He could trip on the sidewalk outside...

My planning is interrupted by grunts of exertion as Arnie bends down on one knee to dig around in his toolbox, his dungarees stretching tautly over his backside, threatening to burst. There's an unfortunately placed dark stain right on the seam in the middle, looking as if he's soiled himself. He certainly smells as if he could have. Willow has the good sense to stay back while he works. I hate the idea of her being in such a closed-off space with this beast. She shouldn't be in the café alone; it isn't safe. I wonder why she doesn't have any other workers?

Think, Freddy, what can we do? Arnie begins testing outlets and flipping breakers. He probably isn't even checking anything, just piddling around to make her give him her hard-earned money for the visit. He takes out a saw and begins cutting away a large section of the wall to reveal some wiring.

"Here's your problem, honey: these are all rotten. You'll need the entire café redone; this is a fire hazard just waiting." He wipes sweat off his face with a dirty cloth and stuffs it back into his pocket, breathing heavily as he rakes his greedy gaze over my golden goddess.

Willow leans in closer to see what he's going on about. I lean in just to be near her, putting my cheek to hers. Her eyes flutter, and she pulls back, grasping her cheek and looking in my direction. She couldn't have felt that... could she? After a second or two of confusion, she turns back to look at the wires. They look brand new. What in the bloody hell does he mean they've rotted?

"How much will that cost?" She asked with her arms folded over her chest. Good girl, stand up to him. "Well, sweetheart, see, that is gonna take a lot of labor hours, so I can't give you an exact dollar amount, but I'll tell ya, you could get shut down for having it this way, that's for sure." Bloody crook. Willow backs out of the storage closet and holds her arm out, gesturing for the farm beast to leave. "I'll have to get a second opinion before I spend a ton of money on fully gutting and rewiring the café." He laughs, his big belly jiggling, "Well, the longer you wait, the worse it's gonna be, I mean, the more likely you're gonna have a fire."

"I'll deal with the consequences if it comes to that. Thank you for your time." He adjusts his clothing and wipes his sweaty face again. "I could make you a special deal, like a special friends discount?" He raises his eyebrows suggestively at her. Oh, that's the final straw, you bastard. We are standing in the open seating area now; Willow is far enough away not to be included in my bad behavior. I backhand the metal toolbox dangling from his meaty, swollen hand. One swift and forceful push, and the corner of the toolbox goes sailing right into his balls.

He doubles over from the blow, gagging and red-faced. Satisfaction washes over me. If I were the old me, I'd have hauled him out of here by the collar and thrown fists in the alleyway. Willow holds the door open for him to slump through. "No, thank you, Arnie, I'll be looking for a more professional electrician to give my business to."

She slams the café door closed and flips the lock. I venture out to the front curb to see that he actually leaves. He tosses the toolbox in the front seat of the truck, then walks around to the driver's side; I lift a screwdriver out of the metal box and into the driver's seat just as he goes to sit down. He howls as he takes a jab right up the ass from the screwdriver, sputtering and cursing as he squirms to remove it from beneath him. Good riddance fucker.

I pass back through the café door to find Willow slumped in one of the chairs, right underneath the spider, uuhhhhh. Her head is in her hands, and she looks defeated. Guilt pumps through my chest; this is because of me. She thinks she's facing financial hardship because I wanted to say hello. I should have been more considerate. I need to be taking care of her. I have to be smarter than this.

A tear escapes and trickles down her cheek. She breaks my heart; braving the spider above, I slip into the chair seat next to her. Snatching a napkin from the dispenser, I dab her tear away. She takes it from me with a pitiful "Thank you," followed by a sniffle. "You're welcome, love, sorry to have caused you trouble," I whisper. Willow's head snaps up, and she frantically looks around the café. "Who's there?"

Oh shit.

CHAPTER 5
WHAT THE FUCK!

Willow

"**O**KAY, *ASSHAT*, I KNOW you're in here!" I ball the napkin up in my fist and shoot up from the booth, frantically looking around the café. I know what I heard. A man's voice, clear as day. "Come out now and you can leave peacefully, but if I have to *hunt you down*, I'm gonna fuck you up!" I muster all the fake bravado I can into the threat. He doesn't need to know that I'm scared shitless right now.

I head behind the service counter, keeping my head up and watching as I bend down slightly and feel for the baseball bat I keep under the register. I know what I heard. I locked the front door after Arnie slithered away, so someone must have slipped in while we were in the storage closet looking at the wiring. I check the kitchen, the office, under tables... I know what I heard. I walk through the coffee shop three more times before I'm ready to put the bat away. What the fuck, am I hallucinating?

I plop back down in the booth with a huff. I'm so stressed out that I'm creating voices in my head. "Hooowwww am I going to afford to have the coffee shop closed to have the entire place rewired?" I lease the space, so ultimately, it won't be my financial responsibility for the repairs, but I would have to close the shop while that's getting done. That would be a big blow to the pocketbook. I have savings for an emergency, but who knows how long it would take, a few weeks at best? And then how long would it take for customers to come back after I reopen? I can't sit here and wallow, though. I need a plan.

Standing up from the booth with a new determination and the residual adrenaline from an intruder scare, I march my ass into the office. Make a list, then mark shit off. Put shit on the list just so you can mark shit off. I'll use the illusion of being productive until I can actually be productive. I am a doer, not a wallower. I am also a complete mess at office organization, where the fuck is a notepad?

I upend drawers until I find one, then slam myself down in the office chair and fire up my computer. Furiously banging on my keyboard, I pull up my lease agreement. I send an email to the company letting them know there may be an electrical issue and asking how to proceed. I'm not about to be left with a huge maintenance bill because I didn't follow proper procedures. Waiting for a reply is going to be brutal, though.

To Do:

~~*write email*~~

Next, I dig around in the storage for fresh batteries and change all the smoke detectors. I unplug everything I can reach and triple-check that nothing is left on. Then I open the register and empty the till. I'll take all the cash home with me each night between bank days until this is settled.

~~*smoke detectors*~~

~~*unplug shit*~~

~~*cash money*~~

I look around for anything else I should consider. I love my decorations, but none of them are irreplaceable. It would suck for sure, but the insurance would help pay to redecorate the place.

Glancing around again, I spy my sweet little statue on the shelf by the entrance. Humphrey isn't replaceable. I'll take him home. I can't explain it, but I just love this little guy so much, it doesn't feel right to risk him.

~~Humphrey~~

"Come on, Humphrey, let's get outta here, babe." I pluck him from the shelf, throw my bags over my shoulder, and head out the back. I don't know why I treat myself like a pack mule. Like, would it totally kill me to make more than one trip, or I don't know, pack around less shit?

Maybe, 'cause I have to take three suitcases just to go to and from work. I use my foot to shut the door to the coffee shop and then squat a little to be able to put the key in and lock it back. Then, I hit the unlock button on my key fob. Only it was actually the panic button, shit. I try to manipulate the key fob in my hand and end up dropping the whole thing, mother fucker. I roll my eyes and tip my head back; this night is sucking hot crusty gym balls.

I could put stuff down and make my life easier, but that's no fun. I squat all the way down and feel for my keys. If I look down or bend my upper body, I'll lose balance and either fall on my ass or drop everything. I scoot my fingertips around in the grass chaotically. Where the fuck are they? Then suddenly, the keys are pressed into my palm, my fingers wrapping around them, oh good. This time, I'm able to get the liftgate open and throw my bags in. I go around the driver's side and rest my coffee tumbler and metal water bottle against the driver's seat.

Whew. I still have Humphrey cradled in the crook of my right arm; his face smashed into my breast. "Sorry, Humphrey, I hope you can breathe right there." I carry him to the passenger's side and buckle him in the seatbelt, nice and snug. I finally get myself settled in the car and crank the ignition. "Okay, babe," I sigh and look over at Humphrey's smiling face, "let's go home." His jovial expression eases my tension a little. I pat him on the head and put the car in gear.

It's a quiet evening. I drive in silence down the highway until I get to the turnoff for my neighborhood. Coming to a stop at the red light, I lean over to fiddle with the radio. My Bluetooth connects and automatically brings up the last song I had been playing.

"Lovers from the Past" by Mareux plays softly from the speakers. I lean forward and crank up the volume. I love the beat of this song. I can get so lost in it, almost trance-like, when I'm working on an art project or something. I pull into my driveway; Mrs. Graham is on her porch in her robe and curlers, having a smoke. I wave to her as I pack all my shit up the front steps.

She is almost always on her front porch, in the same pink fuzzy bathrobe and Velcro curlers, so much so that I'm convinced they might actually be the hairstyle instead of the hair prep work.

"Whatchu got there, honey?" She points her cigarette in my direction. Confused, I look down at myself until my eyes land on Humphrey. He's snugly anchored between my breast and the strap of my laptop bag, his face smiles right back at Mrs. Graham. "Oh, this guy? This is Humphrey. I just got him at the last estate sale I went to! Isn't he cool?" Mrs. Graham grimaces at my chest. She is the most unpleasant, pleasant woman I've ever met. I used to think she hated being my neighbor, but it turns out that's just her face.

"Mm," she says, her cigarette now hanging from between her lips, "good for you, baby, he's a keeper." She looks away, blowing out smoke and waving it away with her arm before flicking away some ash.

"Yeah, thanks, I think so too. Have a good night!" I wave my hand before I lumber inside with my load of stuff.

I set Humphrey down on the kitchen counter. I guess he can hang out there tonight until I decide where to put him. I refill my water from the refrigerator and add a peach tea flavor packet. I'm not sure if this is the same as drinking actual water, but at least I'm getting fluids, that has to count for something, right?

While I stand there with the refrigerator door open, I lament over its contents. I should have made myself a Humphrey Bag-Art before I left work. I literally have nothing in here except coffee creamer, eggs, and half a container of confetti icing. I should have gone by the grocery on the way home, but I didn't have the mental or emotional energy after Arnie's little visit.

Rummaging through my cabinets, I find a bag of animal crackers, grab the icing jar, and plop my ass on the couch. I fucking love this couch. It's purple, and the fabric is so soft. I got it for a steal. Some fru-fru lady had it custom-made, then decided she hated the fabric, so the store was having trouble getting rid of it. Couldn't have thrifted a couch for cheaper than this, and the cushions are magic. I snuggle deeper into them with a sigh.

Like most nights, I click on the TV and surf my streaming service for something to melt my brain. Dipping animal crackers into the icing and flipping through the show catalogue, I settle on a campy murder mystery.

After making myself sick on icing, I clean up my snacks and decide to take a shower. I feel stressed. All this shit with the possibility of having to close the coffee house while the electricity is repaired has my stomach in knots. I need to relieve some of this tension in my body. Maybe a hella good orgasm will help me relax before bed. I turn the water all the way to hot and scrub the shit out of myself.

After I'm done, I step out of the shower and wrap a towel around my hair. Rubbing lotion over my legs, breasts, and ass. I work it in, pressing my hands into my skin for some self-massage. When I turn back around toward the mirror, steam has coated it. The condensation runs down in drips and makes the shape of a heart, how cool! I've never seen water drip like that before. I'll take that as a sign that something good is going to come into my life. Some positivity is just what I need right now.

I towel off my hair and throw the wet towel in the laundry. Missing the basket, it lands on the floor. I have shit aim. Bending over to retrieve it, I get the sensation of something brushing against my naked ass. My hand snaps back to cover my cheek before I spin around to look. I don't see anything that would make sense for the sensation, so I frantically swat at my ass cheeks with both hands to make sure there isn't anything on me. Running back into the bathroom, I grab my hand mirror and pull a Captain Morgan at the edge of the tub. Spreading my ass cheeks and pussy lips, I fish around for anything... a stray hair... towel lint... please God, don't let a spider be crawling over my asshole.

Geeze, I am really losing it. Look how paranoid I've become. I have been coo-coo-ka-choo for the last few months now. Seeing and experiencing things that aren't there. Now I am spread open, digging in my ass and pussy for imaginary critters. This is a new low. Satisfied that I'm not infested with arachnids, I decide a fuck ton of cumming is exactly what I need to calm my brain down.

Kneeling down, I pull my fun box out from underneath the bed. I have an embarrassingly large selection, but when you're perpetually single, you need variety. It isn't like I haven't tried dating; I just never seemed to gel with anyone. I'm always a little too weird and out there for their taste, a little too unladylike. Oh, well, their fucking loss.

I have your basic vibrators and wearables, wands, clit stimulators, plugs, but my current favorite item is my monster dildo and grind mat. This thing is a work of art. I grab it and a vibration wand from the box.

I lay a fresh towel over a pillow, then strap on the grind mat. This thing is so beautiful. The grind mat itself is formed to look like a mountain of bats in ombre purples and turquoise; a large dildo juts up from the base, shaped like a large bat with its wings wrapped tightly around to form the shaft. It's called "The Impaler," lol. A little Dracula humor. The bat's head at the top of the shaft has a little firm nub that hits just right.

I close my eyes and delve into one of my favorite fantasies of a man fucking me from behind. I try to imagine him running his hands over my body. I run the vibrating wand over my nipples, down my stomach, over the tops of my thighs, and over my pussy. With my other hand, I follow the path of the wand, teasing and squeezing along my body.

I reach down and rub the wand over my clit a few times, squeezing my thighs and following with my finger running up and down my pussy. My fantasy man is massaging my breast and kissing my neck and along my jawline.

Once I'm wet enough, I lift my leg and position myself over the pillow and slowly work myself down onto the shaft of the monster toy. The soft silicon of the bat mountain creates an amazing sensation as my clit rubs along it, all the little bumps and ridges stimulating me.

I keep running the wand over my nipples and teasing over my stomach as I circle my hips and tease my clit over the grind mat. As the pleasure builds, I throw the wand onto the bed. Reaching forward, I grab the metal bars of my headboard for stability.

My knees circle in and out as I undulate on the toy, squeezing and clenching my core over the shaft. I'm so gone in the fantasy that I can actually feel the sensation of having my nipples played with and kisses on my neck. And damn does it feel good.

I can smell a woodsy, earthy scent of my fantasy man, his rough, callused hands squeezing my breasts. My breathing is heavy as I start to moan. I love getting loud when I get down and dirty; it makes the fantasy so much more real for me. "Oh, yes, fuck, I love the way you touch me," I grunt into the empty bedroom.

My mind is seriously running away with me because I feel my nipples squeeze so hard that I actually let out a yelp. "Fuck, yes!" I ride my toy like a wild woman, digging my pelvis in and scrubbing back and forth over the grind mat, the shaft as deep as I can get and pressing into that special spot inside.

My shoulders shake as I bear down on the headboard for more support. Fantasy man is squeezing my hips and helping me keep rhythm, "Oh, fuck yes, yes, yes, yes," I chant through gritted teeth as I start to cum so hard. My back bows, and I'm white knuckling the headboard as I grind out the last of my climax, legs shaking. "Fuck, that was so good." I have to sit for a moment as a come down.

The fan overhead is whirling, I'm naked with wet hair from my shower; I should be shivering, but I'm not. Instead, I feel engulfed in warm comfort. Damn, that orgasm did do me some good if it can do that. I should write a review on the website for this monster cock.

When I finally feel like I can move again, I slide off the shaft of the toy with a squelchy pop, leaving strings of thick cum dangling and soaking the bats. I'm dripping down my thighs as I head back to the shower. After the hu-massive cleanup, I can't even bring myself to dress in my pajamas. I fall face-first down onto the bed. I don't even bother covering myself with the blanket. That was exactly what I needed to shake off the stress of the day. I feel warm and cozy, comforted, as I drift off to sleep.

SHRRRRFV, SHRRRFV, SHRRRFY. I'm wandering in the dark, my bare feet shuffling along the floor. The smell of sawdust fills my nose, its fresh-woodiness pungent around me. The dust and debris on the floor collects between my toes.

Shrrrfv, shrrrfv, shrrrfv. The rhythm is steady and harder at the beginning than at the end. I follow the sound. Light glows ahead of me from a lantern; I see the flicker of it on the wall, casting a shadow of a man. He rocks his body with the movement of the sound, forward and back.

I keep going, using my hands along the wall to help keep me oriented. The sawdust between my toes itches, and a coating is forming on my arms, neck, and chest. It's then that I realize I'm completely naked.

I feel alarmed, but my feet keep moving forward, undeterred that I'm moving naked in the dark toward a strange man. But he isn't strange. He is familiar and comforting. I have the sensation that I know him, that I'm on my way to surprise him. When I get closer, the rhythmic sounds stop.

I see the flash of light reflecting from a saw as he moves to place it on a peg. He's shirtless and sweaty, his pants hanging low on his hips, held in place with a worn, brown leather belt. The loose legs of the faded trousers stained with paint and varnish, and holes worn at the knees. The smell of paint thinner seeps into the air, mixing with the sawdust.

I feel heady like I've had a few margaritas. His chest glistens in the lamplight, sweat beads rolling down his muscles. "I know you're there, Sweetling. No point trying to sneak up on me." He grins and turns to face me. The most beautiful human I've ever seen. His chestnut hair is just a little too long, the waves curling over his ears. Gold flecks of his hazel eyes glimmer in the lantern light. I suddenly feel very exposed in my nakedness, unworthy to be in his presence. His grin turns to shock, then awe, as he takes me in.

My insecurities melt away with his expression. "Never mind that, Sweetling. Sneak up on me anytime you'd like." His hand reaches out to my ribs, high enough to brush the underside of my breast with his thumb. His other hand grabbing me by the ass and jerking me roughly to him, the grit of sawdust and sweat on his hand rubbing on my skin.

"Maybe when I finish this commission, I'll make something for us to enjoy together, hmmm. Somewhere to keep you tied up safely, so you can't go sneaking in the middle of the night."

He smiles down at me like the devil, a playful glint in his eye. His lips brush mine gently, filling my heart with euphoria. He ghosts my lips with his, then moves down my neck to my collarbone, licking my skin and squeezing my breast with his hand. He lifts my breast to his lips and sucks hard on my nipple, then nips me playfully.

He laughs against my skin, trailing his hands down my back to squeeze and lift my ass cheeks, my breast still in his mouth. He cracks his palm against my ass and bites at my nipple at the same time.

I wrap my arms around his neck and hang on for dear life to his broad frame. He lifts me by my thighs and sits me on the edge of his worktable. I open my thighs to welcome him closer. He wrenches me closer to the edge, grinding his hard cock into my clit.

His mouth crashes to mine, his kiss is consuming and possessive. I'm drowning in him, I don't need air, I don't need anything, only him. He presses harder against my clit, moving his hips roughly against me, the fabric of his trousers and beast being held back by them driving me to a frenzy of need and lust.

He grabs my breast, his grip rough. He squeezes and slides his index finger and thumb together, closing the space until he's clamped my nipple down between them. His arm bands behind my back, and he ruts against me.

He grabs my hair at the base of my skull and pulls my head to the side as he bites down on the tender flesh of my neck. I cum hard against him, soaking the front of his trouser. I call out in ecstasy, but no sound leaves my mouth.

My alarm blares way too early. I reach toward the nightstand, fumbling for my phone, and hit snooze. I'm not running this morning before work, or ever again for that matter. I can roll over and get another two hours, but I'm plagued by the ache between my thighs from my hot dream.

Fantasy man was a smoke show for sure, and the way he grabbed me, held me... the dream was so vivid, I can still smell a hint of sawdust. I squeeze my thighs together; they're still sore from my escapade last night, damn, I was getting after it like a wild woman.

Must be why I had such a sexy dream. I lay on my stomach and picture him, all sweaty from his work, the ambiance of the lamplight, the grit in his voice when he talked about keeping me tied up. Em, I'd love that. I roll back over and reach back to grip my headboard, imagining being tied to it. I turn my head and spy a red scarf I keep tossed over the end of the headboard.

Threading the scarf through the metal bars, winding it around each of my wrists, I grip the tail ends to give the illusion of being tied up. I picture fantasy carpenter man coming in from work, all sweaty and dirty.

He finds me there, tressed up, waiting on the bed for him. I bend my knees and slide my legs apart, opening myself up for him. A puff of air hits my clit, must be from the ceiling fan, damn, that feels good. I rock my hips, riding the advantageous air flow. I feel it hit my nipples, too.

"Oh, yes, carpenter man, work me like I'm a naughty piece of wood you need to bang into shape." Just then, I get a jolt right to my pussy. I yelp and sit straight up in bed, the scarf falling back between the wall and the headboard. What the fuck? I need to get laid for real because my fantasies are getting way too vivid.

I shake my head and roll off the bed. I'll just take another shower and get ready for work. As I scrub myself over with the sudsy loofa, I realize my hips are tender right over the hipbone. I look down to see four little circular bruises on each side. That's weird, they almost look like fingerprints. I wonder what I leaned against to cause that?

I've always bruised easily; leaning too long against a countertop or sitting in a chair with my foot tucked under me will leave a crazy bruise from time to time. I step out of the shower and move to wipe the steam from the mirror, then finish getting ready for work.

As I wipe the condensation, I catch a glimpse of movement behind me. Startled, I turn around quickly, but nothing's there. Just the shower curtain floating from the way the bathroom vent blows against it.

I laugh at myself for being such a scaredy cat, but I also can't shake the feeling that I'm being watched. I have had that feeling almost constantly over the last few months. I am alone, I tell myself. Although what my eyes see and what my inner self feels don't match up.

As I grab my laptop bag, bookbag, water bottle, and coffee traveler, I look over and see Humphrey staring back at me. He is turned to face me head-on to where I'm positioned to walk out the front door.

"How can I say no to that face? Okay, Humphrey, if you really want to go to work with me today, you can." I swipe him from the counter and tuck him under my arm as I leave through the front door. Same as yesterday, I buckle him in shotgun, and we head to work.

My workday passes without any craziness from the electricity. I was worried about running the toaster oven and the espresso machine at the same time, but that's the only way to get orders out efficiently. I close for a few hours between two and four in the afternoon when business is super slow. This gives me time to check inventory, place orders, and check emails. It's difficult juggling all this by myself. At least Jolie has Krista. I need a Krista.

I've been hesitant to hire someone over the last year. Albert was an awesome employee. He and I were not as close as Jolie, Krista, and I are, but I still considered him a good friend. The customers loved him; he was an excellent barista, and he was kind and thoughtful.

I knew he wouldn't work here forever, just picking up hours between classes at the university. When he was hit by a drunk driver back in the fall, it gutted me. I just haven't been able to think of someone else sharing the coffee shop space with me.

I will have to hire someone eventually, but that will have to wait until I know I won't be potentially looking at shutting down for electric repairs anyway. When I pull up my email, there's no response yet from the building owner. Shit. I was hoping to have something from them, at least an acknowledgement that they are looking into it.

I still have an hour and a half before I reopen. With a huff, I snatch up my keys and head out the back. I walk down the street and turn the corner, and up the next block. Book Ends is just a few feet down this way. I love our little district; we may not be on College Ave or Dickson Street, but we have such a cool shopping area.

I pull the handle of the front door and step inside. Book Ends is a frequent haunt of mine and my friends. We all love, I mean fucking love, to read. I can absolutely devour a book in about three to four days, sometimes less. I guess that could be a testament to how little else goes on in my life, but whatever. I'm happy.

The front entrance typically is a wide aisle that branches off in different directions based on the genre. Today, it's an obstacle course of cardboard boxes filled with inventory to be shelved. Damn.

Mrs. Clermont pops up from under the front counter at the sound of the door chime. "Oh! Willow, sweetheart, I'm so happy to see you." She smiles and greets me.

She's one of those women whose age you can never guess. She is going to look fabulously beautiful until the end of time. Her dark hair is always pulled back in a smooth chignon that showcases a chunky grey section that she pins back with a barrette.

Mrs. Clermont was one of my first regular customers when I took over the coffee shop. It had been a very generic café before. I worried about how my style would be received as I started making the place my own. She gave me so much encouragement, told me I had "Big Book Energy" in the new space.

"I'm so glad you came in, I had ordered a new book for stock; it finally came in, and I immediately thought of you when I was looking at the title and descriptions."

She starts rummaging in one of the boxes at her feet. "Here it is. Look at this." She plops a thick book on the counter; it's probably five hundred pages. The cover art is beautiful: a raven with its wings spread, in shades of wine, grey, and navy. I turn it over to view the description.

It's a paranormal romance about a girl who falls in love with a ghost. A review on the back states, "Edgar Allen Poe meets Harlequin romance. A dark and steamy descent into the madness of love, loss, and redemption."

I have to grin. She's right, this is exactly my genre. "Wow, Mrs. C., this is a perfect pick for me. I'll take it." She shakes her head vigorously. "No, my dear. This one is on the house."

Chapter 6

A Little Taste of Hell

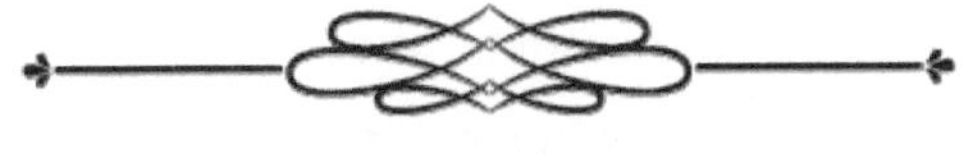

Fredrick

THE SOFT HUM OF water falling from the shower head echoes through the tiny space, punctuated by the intermittent trickling of the drain. Steamy sweat soaks the walls and shower curtain. Have I finally passed on and gone to heaven? Her full breasts bounce and sway as she scrubs and massages every inch of edible skin. I stand in the shower next to her, hypnotized by the flow of frothy soap bubbles as they cascade over her nipples.

Willow opens her legs, bracing her sweet little toes on the edge of the tub while she lathers her pussy with shaving oil. Got to have all our little bits silky smooth, don't we? She drags the razor over the delicate skin, leaving soft silk behind. While she takes a moment to rinse the razor between passes, I seize the opportunity to run my fingers through the smooth skin.

Standing behind her, I lean over her shoulder, entranced by the beads of water dancing over her plush breasts and dribbling off her hard nipples like a sexy little waterfall. My hand brushes over her ass cheek, dipping between and tracing the path over her asshole and up to her clit. Running back and forth through the creases, slickened by the excess of shaving oil.

As she returns to her labor, I hold her open thigh with my other hand, pulling her back to give myself a better view. I run my hand over her soft, soapy skin to her pussy, following her hand through her folds as she rinses herself. The fingers of my other hand still linger on her asshole, rubbing her from the back and the front. What a stolen privilege it is to be touching her most intimate parts. If she could see me, would I still be allowed?

She runs her fingers over her clit and lets a soft, deep breath escape. The steam rises from the shower, suffocating the small bathroom. Condensation cascades over every surface, and the gentle cadence of the shower serenades us. I move around to face her, leaning my forehead into hers and breathing in her breath, trying to gorge myself on the feeling of life I get from being in her presence.

Willow tips her head back against the shower wall as she continues slowly massaging herself. Enjoying the fresh, smooth feel of her pussy as much as I do, I sink to my knees reverently in front of her. Opening my mouth to catch drips of water on my tongue as they fall over the edges of her nipples. I wrap my arms around her hips and under her propped-up thigh. Hugging my body to hers, I press my face into her pussy. Running my tongue through her fingers. She gasps sharply, and I can't help the dark chuckle that escapes me. Yes, Sweetling, enjoy me enjoying you.

I follow her every move with my tongue. As she lifts her fingers to pull back on her pussy, exposing her tender, swollen clit to me, I devour her. The sensation of her fingers and my tongue's joined efforts, sucking her cum off of them and her clit as we work as a team, has such feral urges rising in my chest.

My God in heaven. My cock pulses, I'm lost in thoughts of licking her center like the foil of a biscuit packet when she lets out a guttural moan followed by a high-pitched keening of pleasure, so I double my efforts. Ffffuuuccckkkk. I'm a bloody sick fuck. I shouldn't be in here; I should be giving her privacy. I should be respecting boundaries. I should be wooing her properly. But I can't tear myself away from her. I want to please her like no one ever has before. I want to wipe her brain of all other experiences. I want to plunge myself so deeply into her body, merge myself so completely with her, that our hearts and souls are fused together and neither time nor reality could separate us.

I rise to stand before her. As I run my fingers through the mess she's made between her legs, I whisper dirty words in her ear. Even though I know she can't hear me, my heart begs that she senses my desires for her somewhere deep in her mind. "You're really a dirty girl, aren't you, Sweetling?" I run my tongue up the length of her neck. "Such a contradiction, your angelic features and sweet demeanor, but underneath all that hides a dirty little sex devil, isn't that right?" I say.

I run my other hand over her breast, playing with her nipple, and then down her belly to her hips and over her ass cheek. I continue, "Naughty angel, cumming in the shower while I watch. Letting a perfect stranger lick her dripping pussy and squeeze her nipples while she fingers herself."

I grip her ass cheek hard and grind my palm into her now sensitive clit, enjoying the way her body tightens and the pulsing of her clit against my palm. "All sugar and cream aren't you, Willow? I'd collect all your cream every morning to sweeten my coffee," I lick up her neck again and nip at the vein there. "I'd spread it all over my morning toasts," I grunt. Her fingers wiggle and writhe beneath my palm, her other hand braced tightly against the tile of the shower, her fingertips blanched with the effort.

She picks up her pace and her force as she rides her hand furiously. I grip her ass tighter, imagining that it's me she is filled with, and help her keep purchase and tempo as she rides herself into oblivion. Slipping my hand forward, I wedge my fingers between hers, stretching her inside, desperate to participate in every way I can.

She grinds against her clit with the heel of her hand. Cupping her hand in mine, I guide us, rotating in circles and bearing down on her swollen nub. Her moans have my heart racing and my cock bloody damn jealous of my fingers right now. I tuck my head and bury my face into the soft of her neck, holding her as close as I can while she falls to pieces, her pussy pulsing as a flood of that sweet cream pumps from her body.

We are both frozen in the peace that follows our frenzy. Breaths huffing together, trying to find reality again. I worry for a moment that she might pass out in all this steam. After a few moments, she removes her fingers from her sweet cunt, the debaucherous squelch that accompanies the act has a giant grin splitting my face. "That sounds better than any applause, love," I say.

Her delectable juices, sticky over her fingers, glisten temptingly in the dim shower light. Delicious nectar that has me salivating. Every time I've pined for a custard, a beer, a proper cottage pie... all of those combined could not come close to the desire I have to taste Willow, to keep tasting Willow. I run my tongue over her fingers, gathering her juices as she washes her hands in the shower spray. I suck my own fingers clean next, and God, how the tangy, delicate flavor bursts in my mouth, fuck this is torture. No, I haven't gone to heaven; I'm definitely in hell.

Willow's steps are unsteady as she exits the shower and attempts to dry herself off. The combination of the orgasm and the steamy room has made her lightheaded. I help her with the towel and try to steady her as much as I can. If it wouldn't send her screaming to a priest for an exorcism, I would carry her to bed. The mirror is still completely fogged over. I draw out a little message in the steam that's collected there. A small token of my affection.

Fantasy of a real life with her plays out in my mind. I would be the one washing her up after she cums. Dry her hair for her, carry her to bed, bring her treats. Whisper sweet praises in her ear as she drifts off to sleep...

Instead, I'm following behind her with my arms held out, in case she should fall. When she finally plops onto her mattress, I pull the blanket up and tuck her in. Lingering until she falls asleep, brushing my fingers softly and rhythmically over her hair, rolling the soft tendrils through my fingers. I hum a lullaby deep in my chest while I admire her flushed cheeks and the gentle turn of her lips as she slips into unconsciousness, blissed out by our shower together.

We stay like this for hours; she lies content next to me while I ponder my existence for the millionth time since *the incident*. My feelings for Willow have nothing to do with reason. Why now? Why, after all these years of lament, have I finally found something to hope for? I was enthralled and captivated from the first moment I saw her. As I become more acquainted with the deeper, intimate parts of her— learning the person inside the beautiful exterior— my affection only grows.

Midnight approaches. The early morning hours are when I feel the most restless. The quiet stillness of the world blares regrets at me. What had I done in my life that was so egregious that I should earn this fate? To wander alone for decades, only to find my soulmate in someone I can only love from afar?

Willow is sleeping peacefully and tucked in tight. Not me, though, I'm a mess of thoughts and feelings. I'm blessed to have such unfettered access to this ethereal creature, watching her, being next to her for every secret thought, for every breath, but that isn't enough. I want to peel back everything and crawl inside her soul until I know her on such an intimate level that no one could discern her soul from mine. I can't help but feel as though she belongs to me, that we are destined to be connected. A seductive delusion that I'm more than willing to drown myself in.

Wandering around the house, I take in her most intimate space. Her home is incredible. There are paintings and multimedia pieces covering almost every inch of the walls; no need for wallpaper or fancy paint when you have all this wonder to hang. I lean in closer to one of the pieces. It's an abstract landscape, trees breach the waterline, and their roots sink below. Violet and gold accents define the landscape.

Closer inspection shows a signature at the bottom corner. *W. Nightgood '19.* I see her name repeated on many others. She must have done all these pieces. Her walls are coated in them. Some are framed in decadent gold frames, others are artfully arranged in varied sizes with other eclectic pieces mixed in.

Flowers fill vases across countertops, and color is vibrantly used in every room. Her entire home is like a work of art, everything working together to bring a feeling of life and energy to her space.

Self-expression exposes the intricate and raw parts of her emotions. I wonder who else has the privilege to understand her on such an intimate level. Jealousy flares in my chest at the thought of another man standing here, seeing her like this. I want it to only ever be me. How can it really ever be me?

I climb back onto the bed behind her, wrapping her protectively in my arms as if someone might come in the night to snatch her away. This is home. This is where I want to spend my eternity, next to Willow. Again, I feel the tug of responsibility. If I were a physical man, I would take such good care of her. I would cook her meals and spoon-feed her while she sat on my lap. I'd work my hands to the bone, so she never wanted for anything.

I watch over her as she sleeps through the night. Keeping guard to make sure her dreams stay sweet, and nothing can disturb her. "I swear to you, Willow," I whisper softly into the darkness. What? What can I actually swear when I don't know my own fate? So, I say the only thing I know for certain. "I am yours."

I'm sitting in one of the velvet booths with a couple of college students. They're lamenting their summer courses, and I'm enjoying the juicy gossip about the dirty social sciences professor suspected of being the campus flasher.

Apparently, Ashley was told by Kimberly, who heard from Rebecca, who was told by Jessica, that Sarah Ann was walking down the hallway when Professor Matthews passed her with his fly un-zipped, and he supposedly made a big show of fixing himself while making direct eye contact with Sarah Ann. They can all agree that he has that older "dirty daddy" vibe.

My days have passed this way in a comfortable routine. To my fortune, she has quite an attachment to Humphrey and packs him everywhere. I travel back and forth from work and home with Willow. I spend my time following her around the coffee house, learning all about drinks and helping out when I can, like moving pitchers away from the counter's edge because apparently, she has no idea where her elbows are at any given time, bless her.

As late afternoon descends, business begins to pick up. This is when she needs me behind the scenes the most. So far today, I've prevented a handful of oven fires, saved a couple of bagels from burning in the toaster, and kept the beans topped off in the grinder so she can work more steadily on her orders. How did she manage all this alone?

"I told you, sweetheart, I wanted quarters. I need the quarters for the paper box up the corner." An overly grouchy voice elevates above the typical hustle and bustle of the coffee shop. "You *hipster alternative weirdos* think you can just run a business *any* kinda way. You have to please the customer, or the customer don't come back. Now, I *want* my quarters!" The metallic clang of change hitting the counter punctuates his angry words.

I come from the back, where I was drying coffee carafes, to see the disgruntled customer in question scowling at my Willow. My Willow, Willow who belongs to me, Willow who no one has the right to treat cruelly. She's holding her hands out apologetically to the man and trying to explain to him that she is out of quarters at the moment.

"You don't keep extra change in the back for situations like this? Well! With business sense like that, you'll be closing your doors in no time," he grumbles. "What about in here?"

Before Willow can stop him, he upturns the tip jar and starts shaking out all the contents. Dollars and change spill across the countertop. I start snatching up what spills to the floor, making sure Willow doesn't lose any of her hard-earned money.

"Goddammit." He mutters when he sees there aren't any of the coins he wants in the tip jar either. He's made a mess for no gain and is quickly making an enemy out of me.

"I'm sorry, sir, but most people use a card for purchases these days, so there isn't as much demand for making change." She tries to placate him. "Here's your coffee," she says softly as she slides the to-go cup over the counter to him. Just then, another customer approaches the counter, her hand held out toward Mr. Shit-for-manners.

"I have some quarters." She smiles generously, reaching out her hand with her offering. Shit-for-manners slaps her hand away, and coins go flying across the floor. I'm around the countertop now, placing myself between him and Willow, ready to grab this prick by the collar. Willow crosses her arms and, with a determined expression and her best authoritative voice, says, "Sir, I'm going to ask you to leave, and please never patronize my business again."

Pride has my chest puffing. That's my girl. Tell him where to shove his pocket change. "Oh, believe me, I won't be back, and I'm gonna write a review about how I was treated today!" He nods his head emphatically as if nailing down his threat.

The other customers look on with mixed expressions of shock and disapproval as he makes his way out. And because I can't abide being a spectator where Willow is concerned, I follow him out to the sidewalk. I have to hurry before he gets so far that the pull of the bottle holds me back. As soon as we cross the threshold and the shop door swings closed behind us, I grip my hand around the top of the to-go cup, just underneath the lid. As he lifts it to his lips for a sip, I squeeze, popping the lid off and exploding hot coffee all over him.

He sputters and cusses as he fans his shirt and dances around like a fool. When he reaches for the door to reenter the shop, I clamp my hand down on the knob, pulling it back so it doesn't budge. My face splits in a maniacal grin of satisfaction when I catch his expression reflected in the glass of the door. He struggles, red-faced with anger and effort, but there's no fucking way I'm letting him back in Willow's shop. When he finally gives up and storms off with his sullied clothes and pride, I venture back inside to check on my girl.

The woman who offered her quarters is still at the counter; she mirrors Willow's stance with arms folded over her chest as the two watch the angry customer stomp down the block. "Well, would you look at that. Karma can be a real bitch sometimes." She smiles and shakes her head, then drops her quarters into Willow's tip jar. She holds her hand up to block Willow's protest. "Honey, after a customer like that, you deserve a little extra."

Other customers follow suit, dropping whatever leftover change they had into Willow's jar and all promising to write excellent reviews of the shop to counter anything that dumpster rat might write. Her eyes glisten with moisture at the kindness of her customers. I place my hand on her back, needing to touch her, to reassure her I'm always with her. Her head jerks to look over her shoulder the moment I make contact. Her eyebrows furrow in confusion, but she doesn't move away.

When the shop finally closes for the day, my sweet Willow is exhausted. I do my best to clean up what I can without her seeing. Forgotten to-go cups, dropped napkins, crumbs on the table... I take the disinfectant spray and cloth she's set out to wipe down the tables for her while she's distracted in the kitchen. I let my mind drift into a wishful daydream of a life like this. A life where I'm not invisible. A life where she knows she's mine, just as much as I know I am hers. Working side by side with her, content and peaceful, then taking her home at night to ravish and to hold.

The doors are locked, and the lights are low, creating a secluded and romantic atmosphere for the two of us. Greedily, I let myself drift deeper into the daydream. I'd kiss all of her stress away, rub her body down, and ease her aching muscles. Strip her clothes away and devour every inch of her... doing anything I could to ease her burdens. My chest aches with the desire for something impossible.

She sighs as she stands at the sink, washing the last of the dishes. I spread my arms around her and brace on the countertop, caging her in. Her coffee and cream scent swirls around me. I lean in and press my nose into the curve of her neck, stealing an intimate moment.

She pauses and tilts her head back just a little, inviting me in. All too eager to oblige her, I lean in closer, pressing my chest into her back and wrapping my hands around her front. Her deep sigh of contentment is all the encouragement I need.

I run my hands under the hem of her shirt and over the butter-soft skin of her stomach. Ghosting my touch upward to the bottom of her bra. Her beautiful breasts are a precious bounty under my palms. Her head leans further back, as if resting on my shoulder, her eyes drifting close. I hike up her bra over her breasts, spilling them from the bondage. Just as they pop free, jiggling from the recoil, the spell is broken.

"Oh my God!" she shrieks and jerks her body forward, suds and water splash over us as she overcompensates and her arms dive into the soapy sink. "Mother fucker," she mutters as her wet, soapy hands clammer to pull her bra back into place. Even though she can't feel it, I lean in and press a gentle kiss to her temple, then discreetly grab a towel and wipe the sloshed water from the floor.

Willow makes me want things again. Things I'd convinced myself I didn't deserve. A longing that is so strong I feel like I could burst. If I did, I wonder if I would turn into pure energy and disperse into the universe.

Teasing moments of connection when she senses me are like pins pricking at my heart. I want so badly to interact with her. It's been decades since I even dared to hope to reach someone.

The thought of finality used to tease me; to finally have an end to my suffering existence seemed something to look forward to. I had resigned myself to loneliness and isolation for eternity. Now, the thought of dissipating into the ether and leaving Willow behind feels like despair.

I brushed my lips to hers this morning, and I'm sure she felt me. That's been happening more and more. Usually, my existence is void of any sensation, any sharing like that. Like yesterday, when I reached out to cup her breast and raked my thumb over her nipple. She shivered and then rubbed her breast right where my hand had been. When I tried a second time, there was no reaction, though.

I torture myself with thoughts of her future. Will she keep the bottle for the rest of her life like Edith had, or will I end up cast aside in another rummage sale?

What if she does keep Humphrey? Will I witness her fall in love with someone else? Will I watch their children grow? A mixture of agony and fury courses through me at the mental image of witnessing her body writhe with ecstasy from another man. Before I know it, the lights are flickering around the house. Ominous flashes crash into darkness. Vibration thunders the walls as every mirror, every painting, every book on the shelf shivers with my emotions.

Willow leaps up from the couch where she's been reading for the last few hours. At first, frozen by the change in energy, then she moves to duck underneath the coffee table. I finally wake the fuck up and realize I've caused her fear with my lack of self-control. I try to calm myself, but now it's fueled by my alarm that I've caused her distress, which only escalates the energy coursing from me.

Books begin flying from her bookshelf, pelting Willow the opposite wall. Willow screams as a mirror crashes to the floor and shatters. I rush to her and cover her with my body. I don't know what protection I can give her, but the need in me is too great to ignore.

Holding her does the trick, though. Having her in my arms quells the agony conjured by my imagination of her life moving on without me.

As the energy settles and lights return to normal, only the sound of her panting fills the stillness left in my wake. She slowly creeps out from my arms and out from under the coffee table. How could I be so stupid? Honestly, I had no idea I was capable of conjuring something so violent and untamed. I could have hurt her. Fuck.

She turns a circle as she surveys the mess I've made. "Since when do we get earthquakes in Fayetteville?" She heads outside to the porch to look around the neighborhood. I take the opportunity of her absence to try to put things back in order. It's the least I can do. I right the mirror and return the books to the shelf. She'll be so sad, she loves her books. I check each of them over, I don't think I've damaged any of the covers or torn any pages.

Thank goodness for that. I'm just getting the brush and pan to sweep up the broken glass from the mirror when I hear a blood-curdling scream from behind me, shit.

I turn around to see Willow looking pale and terrified, her eyes locked on the brush and dustpan I'm holding. Double shit, not only did I fuck up and cause this mess, now I've scared the piss out of her while trying to clean it up. I've nothing to do but continue sweeping the glass. The last thing needed is for her to step on any and cut her feet. She backs out of the living room, and I hear the slam of her bedroom door and the flip of a lock.

I continue my task of cleaning up and give her some privacy to recover from what's just happened. After I've discarded the broken glass in the bin and finished tidying up, I pass through the bedroom door to check on her.

She is lying on her bed, the blanket pulled over her head, and the light from her laptop glowing from within the little cave she's made for herself. I slip under the blanket with her and look over her shoulder. The search bar is filled in with a query, *broom sweeps up glass by itself.* She backs the text up and searches *books flying off the shelf,* then again, *to walls shaking for no reason.*

All her searches come back with various websites about ghosts, poltergeists, the occult, ghost hunters, and the most haunted places in Arkansas. "Fuck, fuck, fuck." She whispers. I exhale heavily and rest my head in my hands. Fuck is right, love. My only hope is that she doesn't connect this to Humphrey. If she chucks the bottle in a river, I'll never see the light of day again.

Chapter 7
Poltergeist

Willow

I NEED COFFEE. I close my laptop and slowly slip out from under the comforter I've been hiding under all night. Maybe I can slip into the kitchen unnoticed? I crack my bedroom door and peek through. The coast looks clear, but when the thing you're trying to avoid is invisible...

I take a tentative step into the hallway; there's no stirring from the living room. Maybe it's sleeping? Maybe I hallucinated the whole thing? Maybe I could convince myself of that if the evidence of the broken mirror wasn't still in my trash can.

Last night... I thought it was an earthquake. When it was over, I went outside to see if the neighborhood was okay; everything was quiet. Lights were on in my neighbors' windows, and I could see them sitting on their couches, watching TV or laughing with their families.

Mrs. Graham was on her porch smoking, still in her curlers. She looked at me like I had seven heads when I asked her if she felt the earthquake. When I rushed back inside, almost everything was back in order. For a split second, I thought I *had* dreamed it all, then I saw the broom... sweeping on its own... it paused momentarily, then continued on as if it was the most ordinary thing.

Creeping toward the kitchen on tiptoes, I don't bother with the lights. The less I disturb anything, the better my chances of sneaking past whatever entity I'm now cohabiting with. I slowly open the cabinet and lift a mug from the shelf, moving as silently as possible, careful not to clink any of the other mugs or bang the cabinet door. The closing of the coffee pot lever and the steaming of the water sound like construction equipment right now. Please don't wake the ghost up...

I grasp the handle of the refrigerator and pop it open, pausing to see if I hear anything. I splash a little creamer into my cup. Normally, I would add whip topping, but I think that might be too noisy— as I turn back to get my cup, my elbow catches it and sends it flying off the countertop.

I reach my hands out fruitlessly as if I could catch the ceramic missile, lava-hot coffee sloshing into the air, and I freeze— I freeze because the cup freezes. A breath before it smashes to the floor, it stops, suspended in the air, hovering half a foot from its total demise.

I don't move, I don't breathe, I don't blink. My heartbeat thumps in my ears. The slow rise of my now half-empty coffee mug has my undivided attention as it levitates back to the kitchen counter.

Fuck, fuck, fuckety, fuck! I have a ghost. I have a ghost in my house. I have lived here for three years. How did I get a fucking ghost in my house? This is what I get for being so fascinated with the macabre, old horror, ghost-hunting shows, Dracula.... What did I actually expect to happen?

My feet squeak on the tile floor as I turn my body to face the offending mug. My hands raised to show I mean no harm; I step backward toward my back door. Feeling along the edge of the kitchen counter and the entryway hall until my ass hits the doorknob. I reach behind my back with one hand and slowly turn the knob and slither through the door to my back step.

Once I'm outside, I dash into the backyard toward the large oak tree. Slow in, slow out. I repeat this to myself over and over, trying to prevent the oncoming panic of my new reality.

I think back to all the odd things that have happened to me over the last few months. The constant feeling of being watched, the glimpses of a man just beyond my periphery... the message on the bathroom mirror: *Perfection.*

I press my hand to my chest, willing my heart to return to a normal beat. Well, my mother is just gonna *LOVE* this, isn't she? She thought my vibes were too freaky to get a man as is; having an otherworldly roommate is just the frosting her cupcakes needed. Silver lining: Maybe she'll quit setting me up on dates.

I pace barefoot through the grass, hands on my hips. This is bad. I have a business to run, and this is my home— my sanctuary. I can't let some supernatural squatter turn my life upside down!

Okay, think, Willow, if it wanted to murder you, then you'd be dead already. The cool morning air has goosebumps coating my arms, and my nipples have turned rock hard against my pajama tank top. I can't stand outside half-naked waiting for this thing to leave on its own. The sun is beginning to rise, mixing with the grey of morning to cast a golden hue over my backyard. I catch a glimpse of movement through my kitchen window. Eep! Maybe I can wait a few more minutes.

A few more minutes turned into an hour of waffling on my part. Bouncing between boss bitch mode and I want to pee my pants mode, I'm struggling to make my feet move toward the door.

I have to get to work. The coffee shop is supposed to open soon, and I can't walk there in my pajamas with my jiggly titties on high beam. I need to shower, change, and get my keys.

Scraping my toes along the grass, I force one foot forward, then the other, until I'm an arm's length away from my back door. You can be brave, Willow. I grasp the knob, turn it, and crack the door open.

The warmth inside my house gives a false sense of welcome as I step back into the entry hallway. Aren't you supposed to feel chills when a ghost is present? The quiet is an eerie backdrop to the knowledge that something otherworldly is lurking in my living room.

"Hello?" Please don't answer me, please don't answer me, please don't answer. Nothing. Okay, that's got to be a good sign. Or it's waiting for me to feel confident so it can jump out and get me.

"Just so you know, I do NOT consent to any kind of possession!" I pause, listening to the silence. "I just want to make that *perfectly* clear!" I must be delulu to think that will work. There's a hunk of tourmaline on the floating shelf right as I enter the living room. I snatch it up and squeeze it in my fist.

The spilled coffee in the kitchen has been mopped up when I walked through. The lamps in the living room have been turned on, and the room is pristine, maybe even cleaner than before the "earthquake." I should count myself lucky that my ghost will at least tidy up after itself.

"Hello?" I try again. "Are you still there?" The book Mrs. Clermont gave me scoots on the coffee table. It shifts and rotates toward me, the pages begin to flip open to the spot I left off on last night, and my bookmark turns perpendicular on the page. I venture a little closer to see the line the bookmark is resting under. It's the section of the book where the ghost has written a message to the FMC in the spilled dirt from an overturned flowerpot in her garden: "Hello, love."

I'm grateful when the alarm starts blaring for me to get ready for work. I haven't been sleeping much at night. After the whole book thing, I grabbed a change of clothes and my keys and hauled ass to Dripping. I spent the day trying to wrap my mind around the situation. It had me so messed up that I miscounted my inventory and ordered double the bottles of flavored syrup that I needed. At least I'll have a stockpile of vanilla and white chocolate.

When I got home that evening, it was quiet. I don't know what's worse, seeing a ghost in action or knowing it's here, but not knowing what it's doing. What does it do while I'm at work? Who is it? Or should I say, who was it? And why or how did it choose me?

It's been uneventful ever since the "earthquake" day, with the exception of the footsteps I hear through the night. They aren't the clomping kind you hear on those ghost hunter TV shows; it's more like someone trying to be quiet, so they don't disturb anyone.

I come home each evening and lock myself back in my bedroom for the rest of the night. As if a lock could keep out a ghost, but this one seems to like staying in the living room.

I do the absolute bare minimum to make myself hygienic for work, grab my bags, and rush out the door when the morning comes. I can't wait to be out of this house. I feel like something is following me everywhere I go. I know it's probably just paranoia, but I can't shake the anxiety. I think I catch glimpses of shadows from the corner of my vision, reflections of a person in the stainless-steel appliances, constantly feeling like someone is standing right behind me.

Maybe it's the lack of sleep and all the worrying, but it feels like there is more to do at Dripping lately, too. More dishes to wash and crumbs to wipe. It's taking me almost an hour longer to clean up in the evenings. It feels lonely there, too. I've worked the coffee shop on my own for a really long time now, but something feels like it's missing now. I feel like I'm missing something.

I'm an absolute wreck when Jolie and Krista come into the coffee shop at the end of the day. I'm a shit friend. With everything that went down with Scott and Jolie, I haven't been there for her as much as I should have. Amazingly, everything worked out, and now she has her happily ever after with an amazing fiancé.

We decided to go out for dinner and drinks with the other ladies of the block. Catching up with everyone is well overdue. Sitting on the patio at a large table, drinking margaritas, everyone is laughing and having a great time except me. I'm nursing a double tequila with lime and trying not to fall asleep in my nachos.

Krista elbows me in the side. "Hey girlie, what's on your mind?" I sigh and take a tentative sip of my drink. "I just haven't been sleeping well lately." I smile and hope she moves on, but nope. Krista is a very intuitive person, and my brush-off response won't get me far with her. "Spill it, bitch." She levels her eyes on me and takes a long draw off her tiny cocktail straw.

I lean in really close so I can whisper in her ear. "I think my house is being haunted by a poltergeist." She jerks back from me and shouts, "What the actual fuck?" Great, now we have the attention of everyone at our table *and* everyone on the patio.

All my friends' eyes are locked on me expectantly. Krista looks from me to them and back, silently questioning if she has my permission. I wave my hand outward toward the table. Krista clears her throat and addresses the friend group. "Um, Willow, um…Willow thinks her house is haunted by a poltergeist." Everyone looks at me with varying expressions of astonishment. Multiple sets of wide eyes just blinking back at me.

I sigh with resignation and explain what's been happening. "Uh, I was up reading that book you gave me, Mrs. C. It's really good, by the way, thanks again." I clear my throat and slug back the remainder of my tequila. Holding my glass up, I signal the waitress for a refill, then continue. "Well, I was just getting to a really spooky part when I was interrupted by an unusual event. So, uh, the lights began flickering, and then the walls were shaking, and then books started flying around the room."

No one speaks, waiting to see if there's more. "So, uh, also, before all that happened, there have been a few other strange things. Like, lights flickering at the coffee shop, I thought I heard a man's voice, and things written on the mirror after my shower."

It's the broom story that really gets the shock and awe response. "Where do you think this came from?" Tara asks.

"I honestly don't know. I like all the dark, spooky stuff, but I don't do anything that I think would invite something into my life." The waitress returns with my double tequila, and I knock it back in one go, immediately requesting another. Maybe if I get totally shit faced I can rest tonight without worry.

"Do you need a place to stay?" Jolie asks. I shake my head. "No, guys, I appreciate it, really, but I don't think this thing means me harm. It's just hard to relax knowing something you can't see is sharing space with you."

Krista places a soothing hand on my shoulder, "Maybe you should try to communicate with it? You know, like get a medium or spiritualist to come over. Maybe this thing needs something from you to cross over or some shit like that?"

I had thought about that, but honestly, engaging with "it" more makes me nervous as shit. "I'll think about that." She rubs my shoulder and leans in for a side hug. "We can all come over and be with you, just say the word." I smile at my little group and knock back another tequila. "Thanks, guys."

I stumble up my front porch steps and smash my key at the lock. Fuck, I had waaaaayyyyy too much tequila. Thankfully, Krista and Jolie were able to help get me and my car home, so I didn't have to call a ride share.

Although it took a shit ton of reassuring that I could go home to my haunted house in the first place. I don't want to put any of them out. I'm still stabbing my key around for the lock when the door eases open and I stumble through the entryway; guess I didn't shut it well in my hurry this morning. Oh, well, who is going to rob a house guard ghost? "Honey, I'm home!" I holler into the living room and crack up. You'd think it would be harder to get a ghost than get a man, but here we are.

I plop down on the couch, too drunk to shower or even make it to my bed. This is the first time I've risked spending time in front of my house since the "earthquake," but right now I can't care. Lying back against the cushions, I close my eyes, and the world spins. I'm going to regret this, but that's a tomorrow problem.

Sunlight beams into my eyes like razor blades. I stretch and rub my face into the pillow. I'm lying on the couch with a blanket tucked over me, my shoes have been removed, and there is a glass of water and some aspirin on the coffee table. I don't remember much about what happened after I came home last night, but I know if I got up to get painkillers, I would have gone ahead and taken them, not laid them out like room service.

I sit up with a groan, holding my head in my hands, when I feel a cold, wet nudge against my fingers. Peeking through them, I see the glass of water hovering just in front of my face. This is so fucking weird. I reach out to take it, taking a slow sip as I stare at the nothing who just handed it to me. The pills are next to be offered. "Tank ew," I say as I swallow them. Fuck, I'm getting my hangover treated by a fucking ghost, what the hell?

Pressing the cool glass to my aching forehead, I close my eyes to the burning sunlight for a moment. I feel like absolute shit. I knew that I would, but last night me felt it was necessary. I will not puke; I will not puke. I'm not sure if it's only the tequila making me feel sick or also the turmoil from dealing with a ghost. But I haven't been dealing with it, have I? I've been avoiding it.

I have a bright idea that is either going to help or make this situation so, so, so much worse. I get up and stumble into the kitchen, rummaging through cabinets until I find what I'm looking for. The clang of the metal baking pan on the counter is a little too loud for post-tequila night, and I flinch. Filling the pan with salt, I brace my hands on the countertop, taking some calming breaths. Before I can talk myself out of this completely ludicrous plan, I surge forward with a question.

"Did you cause the earthquake?" I stare at the salt, nothing happens; seconds turn into minutes. This was fucking stupid. As I turn away, I hear the shifting of granules. I look back over my shoulder and fight to hold a scream in my throat as letters begin to form in the salt. *I'm sorry*. Fucking shit. I got an answer. And it's nice, why did my ghost have to be nice? Wait, I don't want a ghost that isn't nice.

What else do I ask? Anything? Do I dare ask for more? My hands are shaking. I feel like I'm going to vomit, and not from a night pounding straight Cuervo. Sweat beads form on my forehead, and I try to slow my breathing enough to get out another question. I'm not sure if there is some kind of weird linking power if I ask a ghost its name. What if knowing its name makes us bonded buddies for life?

"What do you want?" I feel the bile rising higher in my throat, regretting the question as soon as I've spoken the words. *Willow.* I lash out at the countertop, knocking the salt tray into the sink, then flipping the water on. Running to my bedroom, I lock the door and jump under the comforter with my laptop. I need help *now*.

Chapter 8
Madame Ophelia

Willow

My foot splashes in a puddle on the sidewalk, soaking my red sneakers. It's been raining all afternoon. It's like even the weather understands the situation I'm in and is all too happy to help support the aesthetic. I clomp ungracefully down the block, drips falling on my head from overhead signs and awnings. This part of the city is a little questionable; litter decorates the sidewalks of older buildings with grungy exteriors. I pull my raincoat tighter to get some comfort.

Just ahead is the place I'm looking for. It looms ominously in front of me, ready to slurp me inside and tether me for eternity to the supernatural entity that's pining for my soul. Okay, I'm being dramatic. It's just an old grungy building like every other old grungy building on this block. I came here for a purpose, and pussing out isn't going to do me any favors. The neon hand glows in the window with promises of skills to answer all my deepest questions. Challenge excepted, babe.

MADAME OPHELIA

PSYCHIC READINGS AND SPIRITUAL HEALING

A metal sign swings over the door with an all-seeing eye, the red paint faded and peeling, underscored by a message: The answer you seek awaits. I close my eyes and take a deep breath before pushing the door open and stepping inside.

I'm slammed with patchouli. The main wall of the shop is lined with bookshelves housing resources on spiritualism, crystal work, and finding your inner path. The opposite wall has a large tapestry hung that artistically depicts the different suits of Tarot. This place is beautiful and mysterious. I want to be skeptical, but I have to admit the vibe is on point.

There's a long card table that has sectional containers with different oils, candles, and stones with sigils engraved on them. I don't know much about any of this stuff, other than what I've seen in movies, so nothing. They are all so shiny and pretty. Some are meticulously polished, and others are cut roughly into various shapes. From the back hallway, a beautiful and mysterious woman steps through the beaded fringe curtains.

"I am Madame Ophelia. Welcome to my humble shop. I have been waiting for you." She flourishes her hand in the air for dramatic effect. I bet she says that to all the girls, I smirk to myself.

I wouldn't say that I'm a total nonbeliever, obviously, I have an interest in the dark and spooky, but like anything related to things unseen, I know there are definitely charlatans masquerading as the real deal and stealing people's hard-earned money. This shop had amazing reviews on the internet, and apparently, Madame Ophelia is the number one palm reader in the area. I didn't find a single review accusing her of any kind of manipulation. I can't say the same for the other places I researched.

Madame Ophelia is dressed in a boho-style skirt with quilt squares in earth tones and a cream crochet blouse with flowy sleeves. Her full head of tight curls are the most beautiful color of grey, almost like Champagne mixed with strawberries, pulled up in a messy bun held in place by a scarf.

Her earrings have a fringe style, jingling as she moves her head, ethereal little bells that accentuate her mannerisms. "You've been expecting me?" I give her a skeptical look. She might be the most qualified spiritualist I found online, but I'm still unsure. I hold my ground by the entrance, not willing to give any encouragement in case she's one of those people who use body language tells to try and convince you of their paranormal abilities.

"Ah," she says, "you are one of the guarded ones. I understand." She shakes her head knowingly as she comes closer. With her arms folded over her chest, she walks a circle around me, sizing me up. Her index finger presses into her lips as she "mmhhmm's" and "I see's" me. I follow her with my eyes, equally assessing her as she continues to study me.

I'm starting to get really annoyed. I need a professional to help get rid of my ghost, but perhaps this whole endeavor was a mistake. "You know, actually I'm goo—"

"Ah ha!! You are here about a ghost!" She claps her hands together and leans in so close to my face that our noses almost touch. "Tell me— I am right!"

I'm fuming at this point, defaulting to anger over the fear and discomfort that she does know why I'm here. How could someone guess that without so much as a hello or any kind of foundational questions? I'm angry about the truth, and I'm angry that she could see it. Equally pissed off that I need the help and that I hope I've found it. "Yes, I am here about a ghost." I grit out through my teeth.

"Excellent!!!!" She grabs my hand and begins pulling me toward the backroom, beads from the fringe curtain smacking me in the eyeball, I'm pretty sure I just swallowed a moth, too. The back room is smoky with incense, and there's a large round table covered in a deep purple velvet cloth.

A hand on a base stands in the middle, it looks like some type of model with lines and writing all over the palm and fingers. She guides me into a large wingback chair and moves to sit on the other side of the table from me. I half expect her to pull out a crystal ball with a talking head inside.

Madame Ophelia holds her hands out to me expectantly. Thankfully, she reads the confusion on my face and motions for me to give her my right hand. "This is your first palm reading, my dear." I sit up a little straighter, trying to seem more confident. "No, I get them all the time," I lie.

She chuckles at me and clicks her tongue. "That wasn't a question, my darling. Don't worry... all will be explained. It's all right here." She strokes her long nail down the center of my palm. The Madame pulls out a heavy-looking antique magnifying glass, her eyeball looking comically large from my end, and begins inspecting all the fine lines of my palm. Man, I bet Jolie would love that magnifying glass.

"Hmmm, very healthy, I see, you will live a long time. Yes, yes, uh huh, very interesting... ohhhhhhh, here!" She stabs me in the hand with her nail. I flinch, but her vice grip keeps my hand in place. "See, right here, where your heart line and your fate line intersect..." She looks expectantly from my hand to me and back a few times. I shake my head, but honestly, I have no fucking clue what she means.

"You will be reunited with a love from the past, this love is your fate! Do NOT fuck this up."

This bitch is crazy. "Look, lady... madame... this has nothing to do with the ghost I'm here about, and it will be a cold day in hell before I reconnect with any of my exes. I wouldn't wish flies on those piles of shit."

"Ah, but it does, my darling, it truly does." She leans back in her chair and steeples her fingers under her chin, her long nails tapping rhythmically together. "You see, nothing you do in this life, or the next, happens in isolation. Everything is connected through time and space, tethered together, guiding the soul to action." She smiles at me like she knows some big juicy secret about my life. "Now, tell me about your ghost."

Sitting with Madame Ophelia in her back room has gone from 'mysterious psychic reading' to 'cozy time with your favorite aunt.' I'm sipping Earl Grey and spilling my guts about what has happened, starting with that first weird light show at the coffee shop. "Hmmm, yes, yes, that's very interesting. And you say it was cleaning up the mess it made? And took care of you when you got a hangover?"

"Yeah, that's the weird thing. It apologized for the "earthquake" incident and seems friendly, but I don't know where it came from, and I really don't want to spend the rest of my life feeling like I'm being watched. Friendly or not, you know?"

"Mm, I understand. But lucky you that this is not a hostile spirit seeking to harm you. I can do the séance. Perhaps we can find out who it is that has followed you home and help them get the closure they need to find rest." She takes a slow drink from her teacup, her leg crossed over her knee bouncing as she ponders my predicament. "Tell me something, darling. Did anything new happen before the funny light thingy at your coffee house?"

"No, nothing out of the ordinary has happened. I have just been going back and forth between home and work. I don't have much time to myself for other things right now because I'm running the coffee shop on my own for the time being." I slump down in my chair while I think back over the last few months. My days have been like reruns, repetitive and predictable. All the crazy shit happened to Jolie over the summer, but that's all settled now. Man, the summer seems so far away now...

"I did go to an estate sale with my frie— *HUMPHREY*, you mother fucker!" I shoot up from my seat as the realization crashes over me like a tsunami. That little statue man! Of course, everything started after I brought him home. Damnit! I have been packing him around everywhere with me!!

"Who is Humphrey?" Madame Ophelia draws me from my thoughts; I had almost forgotten we were talking. I'm up and pacing, my fist clenched as I settle into the realization of his betrayal. "Humphrey is the name I gave to this little decorative wine decanter I found at an estate sale. All this started the day I brought him home."

After leaving Madame Ophelia's place, I went back home. She gave me a special candle to burn around my house; she said it would cleanse the space of anything nefarious. It smells like spaghetti and has these strange markings carved into it. Apparently, I don't own any actual candle holders; I buy jar candles from the store, so I've never needed one before. The silver lining is that now I'm able to justify purchasing a full-on candelabra.

I'm daydreaming about walking around my home at night with this giant candelabra, clutching my robe to my bosom and calling into the night for my long-lost husband. Okay, maybe I do deserve to be haunted.

I run the lighter over the bottom of Madame Ophelia's candle to warm the wax, then press it down into a thrifted teacup saucer I found above my refrigerator, when the knocking starts. I jump about a thousand feet, frantically looking around for Humphrey. The knocking continues, and then I realize it isn't a ghost knocking; it's my front door.

Lifting onto my tiptoes, I check the peephole and see the only thing more terrifying than getting haunted: my mother. "Hello, Willow, dear." She pushes past me and welcomes herself into the living room, taking a seat on the very edge of a couch cushion like she might contract something if she actually relaxes here.

"Hey, Momma, this is a surprise." It's been months since I've seen her, and we never get together here or at Dripping. I always have to meet her at one of the more gentrified coffee shops closer to the square or some boutique where she tries to dress me up like a doll. Her taste and mine have never meshed. Which is fine by me— to each their own— but it wasn't fine by her.

A memory of us shopping for school clothes when I was young comes flooding back. I can still smell the mustiness of the store and feel the scratchy fabric of this frilly dress she wanted to buy for me.

It's not that I don't think it's pretty, Momma; I just don't think this is my style. I pleaded with her not to buy the dress. *Well, if you don't like it, Willow, then you just don't know what looks good.* She made off from the dressing room in a huff and slammed the hanger back on the rack. She didn't speak to me for the rest of the afternoon.

Differences in taste have ultimately drifted our relationship apart. She's embarrassed by me in front of her society friends. My coffee shop is scandalizing in her eyes, and my personal style isn't feminine enough for her.

"To what do I owe the pleasure of this unexpected visit?" I try to smile and remember my good southern manners. I should give this a chance; maybe hanging out with her in my own space will open the door for a better relationship between us. That hope quickly falls flat with her next words.

"I see you haven't matured in your style choices yet, Willow." She waves her hand around dismissively at the bookshelf. "Still reading all that dark filth and glamorizing the macabre, I see."

"Uh, yeah, Momma, I still like those things." I shut the door I'm still holding wide open and walk into the kitchen where I left the candle. I light it and place it centered on the coffee table in front of my mother. Let's see how well this baby really works.

"Oh, that's an interesting fragrance. What scent is that?" She holds her index finger primly under her nose. "Spaghetti," I say with a big grin.

"Can I get you anything, some coffee or ..." My voice trails off as I look over into the kitchen and see the coffee pot lever open and close, then my favorite cup, a very *inappropriate for present company* cup, float onto the drip tray. I move to sit on the opposite side of my mother so her back is to the kitchen.

"Yes, dear, that would be lovely, you know how I like it." I nod, keeping my eyes trained on the kitchen, "Yes, ma'am, cream and sugar." The coffee begins to pour into the cup, and the sugar and coffee creamer are being floated around the countertop as if someone is actually holding them.

I scamper into the kitchen, leaping around trying to snatch the floating vessels from the air. My new friend thinks keep-away is a fun game, though. I'm torn between keeping my mother distracted from flying coffee service and letting my poltergeist barista.

"Uh, Willow, this décor is absolutely ghastly. How are you ever going to find a man like this? Men like to envision what kind of homemaker you'll be. No respectable gentleman is going to see you as a serious wife and mother like this, honey, honestly." I freeze at her comment. I shouldn't be surprised; it's nothing I haven't heard before. It still stings, though.

I turn my gaze back toward the coffee pot in time to see the floating bottle of olive oil before it douses my mother's coffee.

Fuck, Humphrey, I appreciate the sentiment, but this really isn't the time. I try to head off the coffee cup in question as it floats toward my mother. It's lifted well over my head and out of reach. I jump, trying to snatch it back, but who can win a game of keep away with a ghost?

The cup floats over my mother's shoulder, and she takes it without even glancing up from her phone. Bringing the cup to her lips, she takes a sip, "Thank you, dear. Now to the reason for my visit."

Thankfully, she doesn't look too hard at the cup to notice she is drinking out of a mug with a phallic-shaped ghost on the front that says *Let's play peek-a-Boo!*

"I came over because you haven't been returning my calls, Willow. That's very unbecoming, you know. Mrs. Jeffery, you remember her, she has a nephew who is doing very well as a lawye—"

"Mom".

"—but he is having trouble finding a nice girl to date—"

"Mom".

"— I thought you two would make a beautiful couple, and just imagine it, Willow, he's a lawyer. And doing very well, he's sure to be making partner at his firm in the next few years."

"MOM!"

She finally stops scrolling on her phone and flips it around to shove a picture of a very mediocre man in my face. "I don't want to date Mrs. Jeffrey's nephew."

"Well, why on earth not, Willow?"

She's getting the same defensive expression from all those years ago in the dress shop, the one she uses to shame me into capitulation. I take a deep breath and try to very clearly express my boundaries.

"I have too much going on with the coffee shop right now, and I'm just not in a great spot for dating at the moment." I leave out the part that I am currently cohabiting with a poltergeist. "And, when I am ready, I will find my own man. I don't want to have social connections with your hoity-toity friends muddying the waters of a relationship." I fold my arms over my chest, ready for a fight.

"Well, I have never understood your need to completely reject all the norms of society, but if you want to end up alone... a spinster... with nothing but your gruesome knickknacks to keep you company, you'll never be able to say your mother didn't try to talk some sense into you!" At that exact moment, my mother, who never breaks a rule of etiquette, rips the wettest, bubbliest-sounding fart I've ever heard.

I look at her. She looks at me. I look at her. She looks at me. Both our faces are probably tomato red. She slides forward and rises from her seat. Setting the coffee cup down on the table, she smooths her blouse and adjusts her pearls.

"I thank you, sweetheart, for the coffee, but it seems to disagree with me for the moment. Perhaps I should be on my way." I try not to embarrass her further by bringing any attention to the gurgling sounds coming from her abdomen.

"Always a pleasure, Momma. Stop by anytime," I say as I rise to see her out. My mother, the image of unattainable grace, walks stiff-legged and pinched-butt out of my home, hustling as gracefully as she can in her kitten heels down the sidewalk and slithers into her sedan. I wave from the porch as she peels out into the street.

Closing the door and heading back into my living room, I sigh as the weight of our conversation settles in the air around me. The spaghetti candle flickers and smokes in front of me on the coffee table. I sink into the cushions of my couch and rest my head back, trying to find the answers to all my problems in the dust on the top of my bookshelves.

I know I'll never please her and myself at the same time. I can pursue the life that makes her proud or the one that brings me joy. I've selfishly chosen the one that brings me joy. It's taken years to come to peace with that, but I won't lie and say it never hurts to know what she really thinks about me.

Humphrey sits on the bookshelf across from me, his little face grinning mischievously back. "What you did to the coffee was very naughty." I fold my arms over my chest and give a pointed glare to the little bottle so he knows I'm serious. The flame on Madame Ophelia's spaghetti candle elongates.

"I don't want to hear any backtalk about it. I know she is miserable to spend time with, but she is still my mother. I can't have you poisoning people's coffee just because you don't like them."

The flame dances around as the candle lifts from the coffee table. I watch with my mouth gaping open as the candle floats through my space, just as Madame Ophelia had instructed me to do. The candle that I thought would diminish his presence is nothing to him. Through the kitchen, the living area, the laundry room, my bedroom... he doesn't miss a square foot. I try not to react, worried he might decide to burn my entire house down.

Gracefully coasting through the air, the candle approaches me and tips sideways, letting wax drip over the surface. When he's done, the candle returns to its place on the coffee table with a heavy clank, and the flame snuffs out. I shift on the couch, my eyes frantically searching the room. I can't find any other signs of where he might be or what he's doing now.

My vision shifts back down to the spilled wax on the coffee table. It isn't just a chaotic mess dripped over the wood. It's a message. *You deserve better.*

Chapter 9
Regret and Resolution

Fredrick

I HAVE MUCH TO regret in my life. Some of it is my own doing, and some of it came from the absence of opportunity. I've had decades to dwell on all the things I wish I had done differently. I haven't fallen into melancholy to this degree since the beginning, though. Yes, sadness comes and goes like the seasons, but the intensity... Energy balloons in my stomach, itching to break free.

Stagnation has plagued my years... until now. My feelings toward Willow, a nascence of possessive obsession, are volatile and gut-wrenching. She's pulled me from the mire to disentangle my soul from the black, torturous void. But my inability to control myself when it comes to her threatens to ruin hope and thrust me right back into it.

The smell of the garage brings me back to the past, and the scent of the wooden shelves makes me itch to build again. I miss creating. I miss the hard, honest work. There's a unique satisfaction in taking raw material and turning it into something that's not only functional, but into something beautiful. I had once dreamed that I could perfect my craft enough to have a small furniture business.

I was on my way too, thinking the promise of my success would help ease the change in social status Isabelle would experience when she married me; our love would soften the rest. There's one regret. Affections wasted on a sour endeavor that was doomed to rot from the start.

I run my hands over the line of tools laid out, screwdrivers, hammers, files... I should never have fallen for Isabelle. With the decades I've had to analyze what happened between us, I see she only used me for sex. A rebellion against her parents, maybe. Selfishness wrapped in a pretty package.

I can still smell her perfume; a memory that once haunted me with heartache now raises bile up my throat. She never wanted me to touch her hair; afraid I might smash down the curls she pinned in place. Never wanted me to kiss her too passionately because her lipstick would smear. Everything centered on her appearance, her status. I was so blind. I can hear the cackle of her laughter the day I asked for her hand.

My fingers roll the ring around in my pocket again, a forever reminder of how close I came to squandering my only heirloom from my late mother on that selfish bitch. *"What is this trinket, Freddy? You can barely even see the diamond?"* My chest still gets tight with the memory. It's the shame I felt, the inadequacy that drove me to the rash action that forever changed my life's course. Another regret, that I allowed myself to feel diminished by someone like her. Someone who valued materialistic treasures over substance. Wealth and societal standing are fleeting. A façade that can't hide the cracks beneath forever. What does it truly gain you if you don't have passion or kindness…?

I grip the handle of the hammer on Willow's garage shelf, squeezing it in my left fist to keep me grounded in this present. I miss the weight of a tool in my hand, the burn in my arms as I sanded and carved. I set it back on the shelf and turn to look at my bottle.

Humphrey, as Willow calls it. He smiles back at me like he knows the punchline of this cosmic joke I call existence. I suppose he does. But he keeps it to himself, always. Never giving anything away.

She's banished me to the garage. Or at least she thinks she has. After that candle she brought home didn't evict me, she decided to move Humphrey out of her house, using a pillowcase to handle the bottle. Probably wise; just speaking from experience. Even though I can still roam her property freely, this is a sign of clear rejection. The hope I let fester in my heart, foolish as it was, is now turning toxic and pustulating

Hope. Fuck hope. It has the power to lift you up and tear you down to your most vulnerable. It makes you desperate. I am desperate. Desperate for a woman who, again, isn't in my station. Ha, I laugh bitterly at that. I truly believed I had a chance with Isabelle, despite the societal differences. Instead of learning my lesson, I've gone even more mental, a ghost trying to win over a living woman.

Again, my thoughts quickly spiral to the inevitable hurt of watching her move on with another man. The audacity that I, a phantom being, would have any claim on a living person. Her life will change, she'll go on to achieve goals, find love, chase her dreams… While I will remain stagnant and out of reach.

Cans of paint and some roller brushes come tumbling from the shelves above me. The walls of the garage shudder and groan under the pressure of my covetous passion. Running my hands through my hair, I seethe with feral rage at the mental image of another man's arms around Willow, whispering loving words in her ear as she drifts to sleep... It should be me!

The metal of the roof vibrates, and the walls shudder louder. The roar in my ears matches the roar of the energy that rushes around me, threatening to pull the small building down.

I crouch down and press my hands into my eyes. Trying to stop the devastating ache that burns in my chest. Something is very wrong with me. I've never had this kind of power before, this untamable surge of destructive energy. I'm drowning in the intense anger and frustration of my plight. Fuck me and my stupid impulses that day. I've cursed myself for eternity with no hope of getting out. No hope of a real human connection again. Destined to exist adrift in the in-between.

I brace my hands on the shelving, face to face with that little villain whom I have come to loathe over the decades. He smiles back at me, "Why won't you tell me your secrets?!" I slam my hands into the shelf. "How do I overcome this?! What could **YOU** possibly gain by keeping me a prisoner?!" My knuckles blanch with my grip on the wood as I fight the energy. "Fuck you! Fuck your magic, you devil!"

The garage rattles and shakes, vibrating with my rage. I want to smash this fucking bottle to pieces, then maybe I could pass on. Something other than this. I reach for it, ready to bash it to utter bits! Then the sweet, angelic face of Willow passes before my eyes. How could I ever leave her?

I set the bottle back on the shelf, lingering my vice-grip hold on it while I pant and shudder from the residual madness. The roaring dies down, and the small garage returns to stillness. When I find the self-control to release the bottle, I stagger backwards and then through the garage wall into the backyard. Slumped against the large oak tree with my head in my hands, I try desperately to slow my breathing. I hope to God that my outburst didn't cause any chaos inside the house.

I need to go in and check before Willow gets home, but I'm rooted to this spot, drifting in and out of memories of the last eight decades and all the opportunities to experience life I missed. None of them can stand up to being with her. And I don't know where that leaves me.

It's late evening when the door finally clicks with the opening of the lock. This is the part of the day when I feel like I can breathe again, when I feel whole again. When my Willow returns home. Being left behind while she goes to work is almost unbearable.

She's got every bag she owns draped over her shoulders, two travel cups, and her cell phone pressed between her ear and her shoulder.

"Momma, if I say yes, will you promise this is the last time?" she begs into the phone. When her mother was here, she was peddling Willow out like a prized mare for breeding.

"Fine, but this is the last time I agree to this... okay, yeah, TONIGHT! Momma, that is not enough time— erhu, fine. Yes, I'll be ready... thanks, love you too.... Yes, Momma, I know how to mind manners— bye."

Willow slams the phone down on the kitchen counter as she shrugs off her load. "I am too damn old for this matchmaker shit!"

She heads off to the bathroom, turns the shower on, and then goes to her closet. A date, then. It's already begun. Will she enjoy his company? Will she accompany him home? I can't imagine it going poorly. Who wouldn't fall enamored under Willow's spell?

I sit on the front porch like a sentry. I can't watch her get ready. I can't watch her shave her body smooth for another man's touches or rouge her lips for another man's kisses. This is the inescapable hell I had feared but resigned myself to. While I sat by the tree this afternoon, I came to the conclusion that this was worth the time I would be with her. The pain was worth the payoff, and pain it is. The setting sun blazes the clouds. The colors are like a fire consuming my insides as darkness descends on my lost soul.

Soon after dusk, an expensive car rolls down the street and parks in front of the house. He honks the horn sharply. Prick isn't even going to come to the door. I bet he didn't even bring her flowers. She deserves so much better. I hang my head into my hands, trying desperately to hold the crack in my chest together long enough for Willow to exit the house.

I can't ruin her chance for happiness. If there is anything that matters more than my passion for her, it's my desire for her happiness and well-being. Focusing on her, that's what holds the damn.

Mrs. Graham comes out onto her porch, dressed in her uniform of bathrobe and curlers; the glow from her cigarette is the only light emanating from her porch. She takes a long drag, releasing the swirls of smoke into the night air. Grey on black tendrils that snake in a melancholy dance, matching my mood.

The door opens, and Willow steps out onto the porch. I feel like someone has taken a dull knife to cut out my heart. She's so beautiful. Her hair flows over her shoulders in silky, soft strands. She's wearing a simple black dress, the neckline falling just off her shoulders, showing off her neck. I'm tormented by the thought of him pushing her hair back and licking at her pulse the way I long to.

Her creamy vanilla scent floats past me as she descends the steps. He doesn't exit the car to help her in, barely waits for her to close the door before he pulls away from the curb. I feel like my heart is being dragged behind it down the street.

"Play the long game, baby, that's what you do for the one that's worth it." Mrs. Graham's voice drifts from next door. I look over to see her stub out her cigarette and go back inside. I don't know who she was talking to, but I'll take that advice as well. I can play the long game, after all, I've nothing but time.

I busy myself around the house while I wait for Willow to return home. Caring for her needs calms the storm in me. I can't sit here and dwell on whether she is laughing at his jokes or if her body is under his hands. A glass shatters in the cabinet behind me. Fuck, that's the third one I've broken. Get yourself together. She can't come home to my chaos and no drinkware.

Her schedule has gotten more and more tiresome as of late. Not only is she running herself to exhaustion manning the coffee shop on her own, but now she is afraid to be at home. Even when she is here, she won't rest. The guilt of what I've done to her guts me. I never wanted it to be this way.

I do whatever task I can find that will help make her life easier, but won't stand out that her ghost has meddled in her life again. The woman really needs a keeper, though. I make my rounds through the house. Unplug the curling iron and change over the wash, so it's finished in the dryer by the time she gets home. That's my favorite chore because I get to handle her pretty little knickers. I enjoy handling the dirty ones even better.

She and her friends are planning a day at the market, and she's been wandering around the house mumbling things she needs to remember to put on a list. I've been putting them down for her, mimicking her handwriting as best I can so she doesn't get spooked. I want to make her life easier, take care of her in any way I can.

My thoughts drift to Edith. When her mind left her, I followed her around the house, making sure she didn't set the place on fire or cause herself harm. I took care of little tasks to help keep the place tidy. It was a fine line, trying to be helpful and keep things looking untouched. When she finally declined to the point she needed full-time nursing care, I was forced to face my utter uselessness, again.

I rummage through the fresh laundry for clothes and find Willow's favorite band t-shirt and spandex shorts, and drape them over the top of the pile so it will be an easy grab for her when she flies out of bed in the morning. Coffee pod next to the pot, water added, her favorite cup waiting to be filled.

It's getting late, and my insides churn with the worry that she may not come home tonight at all. What if she chooses him? What if she's walking into his home right now? Allowing him to remove her dress from her pretty shoulders and run his hands down the curve of her back to her plump ass— a crash from the bathroom cuts through my suffering. The shower curtain has fallen into the tub, and the wand is dousing the room in cold jets of water. Fucking perfect. I turn the nob to cut off the spray and work as quickly as I can to right the curtain and mop up the room. I hope I haven't ruined any of her beauty products.

I'm throwing the wet towels into her washing machine when the hum of an engine and the glare of lights through the front window indicate a car has pulled up. It's almost midnight. I pass through the front door to the porch, unable to help the joy and relief I feel with her return. She didn't stay with him; she came home. She came home to me...

As I cross onto the porch, Willow's body passes straight through mine. Hurrying to the door to place her key in the lock, tears streaking down her beautiful, full cheeks. She never looks back.

Futile. That is what this is. As long as I'm with her, I'll never be able to control myself. As long as I'm with her, I'll never be able to see her as anything but mine.

I turn toward the prick who still hasn't exited the car. Resolved. Committed. Vengeful.

As long as he lingers on the property line, I can reach him. In a flash, I've seated myself in the passenger seat of the car. He's texting another woman about a hookup. Telling her about his sour date with a "freak." I turn the radio all the way up to mask any screaming and rip the key from the ignition. I don't want him to leave our little meet and greet too soon.

He's too slow to react, mouth gaping open at the radio, he's frozen and confused. Taking his phone from his hand, I slam it into his face a few times. Just until I hear a satisfying pop. Blood bursts from his nose, ruining his crisp white shirt and silk tie. "What the fuck?" He holds his face in his hands, and blood pours through his fingers. He blindly searches the console for something to wipe the mess with, but he can choke on it.

I take the key I've pulled from the ignition and drive it into the back of his hand. He screams in pain and jerks away, pulling his hand into his chest. While he whines and cries in agony, I wrap the seatbelt around his neck, ready to squeeze the life from him, but I don't because I don't want Willow to have to explain her dead date in front of her house to the police. But I can take him damn well close to death. So close that he has to fight the urge to vomit if he so much as thinks about this night. So close that he learns what happens when a gutter dweller tries to sully an angel with his rot.

He wheezes, struggling for breath, and piss leaks from his cock. He scratches and tugs at the seatbelt with no success. It doesn't take long for the humidity in the car to rise as he struggles and huffs, fogging the glass.

I reach across his trembling body to the driver's side window. Streaking through the fog, I write, *She's Mine.*

When I return to the house, Willow is lying in bed. She's showered again and dressed herself in cozy clothing. A few short hours and she'll need to be up for the farmer's market. I told myself I'd keep my distance, stay hidden so she would be more at ease. But the soft sounds of tears can't be ignored.

I slip into bed behind her. Wrap my arms around her belly and under her head. She stiffens at first, but then relaxes into me. A heavy sigh escapes her lips, followed by a shuddering breath and a fresh wave of tears.

"You are right, I deserve better..." I pet her hair as her breathing evens out and she drifts off to sleep.

"Yes, my love, you deserve so much better." Better even than me. As bloody possessive as I feel, I know it's selfish. I could never give her what she deserves. What she deserves is a man who can truly be by her side. Not to be haunted by a bastard like me.

And so, I swirl in the torrent of my conflicting emotions once again. I can't stay, but I can't give her up.

CHAPTER 10
FREDDY

Willow

DRIPPING HAS BEEN CRAZY busy this week, and to top it off, the girls and I decided to have a booth at the farmer's market in the square. I don't know what I was thinking, committing to something extra. I've been spending every moment of free time planning supplies and fixing up my menu board.

I wanted to have a few new drinks and food options as specials at the market. It's been a ton of work, but at least I'll be hanging out with my girls for the afternoon. I need some quality friend time after my enlightening visit with Madame Ophelia and my terrible date.

The crisp and breezy fall air is normally soothing for me. I wait all summer for the break from the sweaty heat to the milder temperatures. This is the perfect vibe for the market today, but every time the gentle wind blows, it gives me the sensation of expectation. Something brews in the air ominously. I try to tell myself it's the stress I'm feeling, but somehow I know there is more to it.

Jolie's fur baby, BB, lies carelessly under the shade of the card table. The only concern on her mind is catching any crumbs a passersby might drop. I'm jealous of her. I'm jealous of Jolie, too, if I'm being honest with myself. She has a good man who adores her now. Isn't that what we all deserve? A person who appreciates who we are on the inside? I'm never going on another date set up by my mother.

Mrs. Jeffery's nephew. What a piece of shit he turned out to be. I knew it wasn't going to go well when he didn't open the car door for me. Then, he didn't even look up from his phone as I sat down and buckled my seatbelt. He kept texting while he scolded me for being late. I wasn't late, though. If anyone was late, it was technically him. He pulled up to my house seven minutes later than the expected time. I wouldn't care about that, but he sure did and managed to make it my fault.

When my mother called to "ask" me if I would go out with him that evening, she had already committed on my behalf. I only had about half an hour to freshen up after working all day. I think being on time and looking hot was pretty damn impressive on my part.

The evening only got worse from there. The restaurant was nice, swanky. Weird violin music pumped over the sound system. He stared at my tits the entire meal, even though I wore a dress with a modest neckline. He even asked me how big they were while I was in the middle of telling him about the coffee shop I own.

Yeah, I heard you were into freaky shit. How big are your tits? They gotta be like double D's, right? Mmmm, I bet guys like to squeeze 'em around their cocks—

Excuse me? What kind of question is that for a first date?

Oh, come on. I looked you up. This is never gonna go anywhere, surely you know that. How would that look when I make partner at my firm? Shackled to some freaky chick who likes gory shit and waitresses for a living. I need a woman with a respectable career. But hey, we can still have fun in the meantime, am I right?

This is unbelievable. No, we cannot still have fun. I'm not a waitress; I am a business owner, but even if I were a waitress, all jobs deserve respect and add value to society—

Look, I've brought you out to this nice restaurant. I bet you don't get to enjoy the finer things very often, so maybe you don't realize what kind of money I'm putting down on you tonight. you need to reciprocate—

Thankfully, the waitress came over at that moment and cut him off. I passed her my credit card and asked to cash out my half of the bill. No way was I leaving with him thinking I owed him anything. I didn't continue arguing with him because I didn't want to burst into angry tears in the middle of a five-star restaurant. He ate in tense silence while I sat stone still, digging my fingernails into my palms to keep my emotions under lid. Despite being pissed off that I ended the evening early, I still had to fight off his groping hands on the ride home.

He has a point, though. It's what I've always experienced with men. I mean, you can only have so many of the same encounters before you come to terms with the fact that you are the common denominator.

How much more proof do you need that you are a total freak and will never have a normal romantic human connection than that a *ghost* held you all night while you cried about another failed date with a human man? And what does it say about men in general that a dead one has more emotional intelligence than one with a pulse?

I feel like I'm losing my mind. As much as I want my poltergeist problem resolved, I have to admit, he's growing on me. Maybe being a spinster with a paranormal roommate who will cuddle you when you're sad isn't that awful of a life. And he knows how to work a coffee pot and a broom, two solid green flags.

I watch people wander around the square, buying fruits, vegetables, and art. Oblivious to all the supernatural energies that could be surrounding us right now. Since meeting Madame Ophelia, all I can think about is that anywhere we are, there could easily be an entity lurking over our shoulders. Silently experiencing life right alongside us, how many times have you gotten a chill out of nowhere? Ever felt like you needed to look over your shoulder, like someone was watching you? I had always brushed those feelings off; never again.

And what is it about me? What unique cosmic vibes do I give off that the universe chose me to connect with a ghost? How old is he? How many others has he tried to connect with before me? How many failed attempts to pass on has he gone through? Shit, that must be so discouraging, living for unlimited years trying and failing at the same goal of eternal peace. The thought makes my heart sad.

"So," Krista's voice breaks through my thoughts. "Where are we in the ghost saga? I need an update." I take a moment to help a customer before answering her. "Uh, well," I clear my throat, "as it turns out— so funny story— Haha." I turn to face my crew and the realization I've come to.

"Remember at the estate sale and I found Humphrey, and y'all were all like *Hey, don't open that wine decanter because there might be a ghost in there*, well...Tada!!!" I do some jazz hands for effect. My friends blink back at me in shock. Thankfully, I know they believe me already about the paranormal activity going on, or I would be freaking out right now that they'd have me committed.

"Oh, my God, so there really was a ghost in that bottle?!" Krista almost spits her drink out. Jolie puts her hand on her chest and gasps, "What are you going to do, Willow?" I shuffle my feet before I come clean. "Well, right now, I put Humphrey in 'timeout,' so to speak. He is out in my garage. I moved him out there once I made the connection, and things have calmed down some, or at least I feel more secure in my home. I also went to see a psychic."

Well, after last night, I figured out that moving Humphrey outside actually did nothing to keep him out of the house, but maybe he got the message that he was seriously freaking me out.

"Oh, give me the details. I've always wanted to have a reading done. Was she legit? Was it spooky cool? Did she tell you your future????" Krista plops her ass down in a camping chair with her little travel blanket for story time and peppers me with questions. Another customer stops at the booth for some hot chocolate and a cupcake. I wait until they are out of earshot before continuing.

"All of the above, although nothing quite as straightforward as you would think." I give my best Madame impression and quote her "...Nothing you do in this life, or the next, happens in isolation. Everything is connected through time and space, tethered together, guiding the soul to action..."

"Wow, that is so freaking deep dude, when are you going back?" I shake my head at Krista and shrug.

"So, she has offered her services for a séance to try and talk to Humphrey, but I don't know. I'm nervous to go to that extreme. Can't other spirits hitchhike on a séance? What if, instead of fixing one ghost problem, I end up with multiple ghost problems? And anyway, Humphrey seems to be just fine hanging out in the garage."

Krista pouts at me, "I don't know, Willow. I kinda feel bad for Humphrey. He went from living in a dusty attic to palling around with you everywhere to being shut out again. You ghosted a ghost, babe."

Well, when she puts it that way, I feel like a total bitch for trying to shut Humphrey out, even if it didn't really work. I wonder if I hurt his feelings. Now, thinking about last night makes me feel super guilty. She's right; he's been nothing but nice to me, even if this is a bizarre relationship. I hug my arms around myself, thinking of his embrace last night. I was hurting and raw, and he was there, warm and comforting. He didn't want anything in return.

What if I view his actions from a new perspective? The lights flickering could have been a friendly hello, and he leaves me sweet messages on the bathroom mirror. He stood up to my mom. Okay, the "earthquake" thing was extreme, but he did clean up his mess. Could everything he's done be from a place of care and concern? Call me selfish, but I don't know if I want to give that up just yet. How do you explain to future boyfriends that you have a ghost as a roommate? Would there be future boyfriends if I kept a ghost for a roommate? "Uh! I don't know what to do!"

"I know!" Krista leans in close and motions for us to do the same. "Let's talk to Humphrey ourselves. Like, we could use a spirit board and try to find out what he needs."

I look back and forth between my two best friends. "I don't know, Krista. That still makes me really nervous." She swats my thoughts away with her hand.

"It'll be fine. I think I have one in my garage. I'll bring my board over tonight, and you, me, and Jolie can talk to Humphrey," she says like it's already decided.

"Why do you have a spirit board in your garage?" Jolie asks.

"It's from high school; I bought it to freak my parents out. I've never used it, but I've always wanted to try. This is perfect," she says.

I want to help Humphrey, I do, but also… maybe my attachment to him is a little stronger than I let myself believe? Put aside the risk of attracting something that's spiritually aggressive. What if Humphrey says he wants to move on? What if he tells me exactly what to do to set him free? Do I want that? I'm hurdling full speed toward a choice I'm not ready for.

Oof, my back is killing me. Hauling the coffee carafes and food coolers back into Dripping has me sweating like a pig. Events are fun, but cleaning up afterward is a total bitch.

I put some music on the overhead speaker to help make my tasks a little more tolerable. The sink is overflowing with soap bubbles, and I'm scrubbing away at my utensils and containers, bopping to some 2000s hits when my playlist switches over to a moodier list.

The sad longing of the lyrics brings me back to my hurtful thoughts from earlier in the afternoon. I scrub angrily as I relive my disastrous date night. I reimagine the night, only this time I call him scum and throw my wine in his face. Then, I walk out of the restaurant to the applause of the other patrons.

If I had done anything so dramatic, I would have caught so much shit from my mother, though. Appearances above everything else. As if on cue, my phone chimes with her ringtone from the counter next to me. A quick glance and I see the preview of a text from my mother asking about my date last night. I know she has her hopes sky high that I would come home last night engaged and pregnant.

The slow and soft entrance of the new music is broken by the rattle of the front door. Pausing my scrubbing, I reach up and bump off the sink spray with my wrist, bubbles dripping off my hands. Listening again, I wait to see if the sound is repeated.

I've gotten used to random sounds at home, but I didn't bring Humphrey with me... When nothing happens, I dry my hands off and walk toward the main seating area of the shop. It's not uncommon for people to try the door when I'm here cleaning. They see a few lights and think I might be open.

As I round the counter, I have a better view out of the front glass of the shop windows, they are slightly tinted so customers don't get scorched by the sun in the summertime. I can see out much better than anyone can see in.

It's that odd customer from a few days ago. He likes antiques and left his coffee on the counter. He's got his face close to the window, cupping his hands around his eyes. Something about him gives off a negative vibe. I don't want to deal with him while I'm here alone.

He backs away from the window and tries the doorknob again, but not in a 'is this unlocked' way; it's more like a 'can I get this open' way. Before I can decide what to do about this, he stops and walks away. I wait a few minutes to see if he returns; when he doesn't, I double-check the locks and the alarm.

Frantic pounding threatens to break down my front door. I jump at first, flashing back to what happened at the Dripping earlier, but then get my shit together to let my ludicrous friends inside. Krista is waving a bottle of silver Cuervo in one hand and blasting the Ghostbusters theme song from her phone in the other. Jolie saunters in behind her, holding a spirit board overhead, making an ambulance sound along with the melody.

They parade past me toward the living room. "Bitch! I hope you had the forethought to put shot glasses in the freezer!" Krista calls over her shoulder.

I lock up the front door and follow the sound of chaos into my kitchen. They are making themselves at home as usual, pulling out salt, knives, a cutting board, and my bag of limes. Tequila has always been our liquor of choice.

It started out as bragging rights when Krista and I went out to the club because just the smell of straight Cuervo could make a grown man vomit in his mouth. But we could knock it back like water and still get up and girlboss the next day. Jolie has always been more of a wine girl, but exceptions can be made when we are all out together.

Krista turns toward me, lifting the bottle right to my mouth and pouring before I even have time to fully open up for a shot. I choke and almost snot tequila out of my nose, fuck that burns. I laugh hysterically as I try to recover. "Girl, we gotta get loose before we start conjuring the tall, dark, dead, and handsome," she says.

"You don't know if he's handsome. Or tall. Or dark, for that matter," I counter as she takes a shot herself, straight from the bottle.

"A girl can dream," she says. I pull the bottle away from her and set it on the counter next to where Jolie is cutting limes into small slices. "Why did I freeze shot glasses if you are just gonna drink from the bottle?" I laugh.

We settle around the coffee table with the spirit board and the tequila supplies in the middle. Humphrey stands proudly right next to the bottle of Jose Cuervo. My buzz can't dampen the feeling of trepidation. God, I hope we don't make things worse by doing this. What if Humphrey gets pissed at us?

"Okay," Krista shouts, already a little shitty from tequila, "spooky drinking game... if you say the word *fuck*, you drink. If you say, *I wanna suck ghost dick*, you drink. If you scream like a little *beeeaaachhh*, you drink." I'm grateful for her lighthearted approach; it's keeping me grounded right now.

The board is decorated in varying shades of dark green and burgundy, outlining a beautiful moth in the center with floral patterns on its wings. Gold embossing inscribes letters and numbers across the face of the board. The glass eye of the planchette stares right back at me. Will this even work? I do think getting some answers is a good thing, but who knows what could be waiting for us at the end of this night?

"Okay, bitches, repeat after me, *Let's fucking talk to a ghost!*" In unison, Jolie and I repeat the words, Jolie's much more confident than mine, as Krista pours us all another shot.

My hands are super sweaty as I fight to keep my fingers placed on the planchette. It slithers across the board, inching closer and closer to the word yes. "You bitches better fucking swear on your fucking life that y'all aren't moving this fucking thing on purpose," I say through gritted teeth. Krista grins manically as she stares at it. "When we take our fingers off, you have to take three shots!"

The question, *Are you there?*, hangs in the silence around us as we dare not even breathe until the planchette reaches its destination. Holy mother of pearl, why did I agree to this?

"What's your name?!" Jolie shouts like she just made a new bestie, and I want to run screaming into the night. The planchette scrapes its way down the board, the sound sending ice-cold chills down my spine. *F... R... E, D.... R......... I.................. C.....................*
K.

"Ohh, *Fredrick*, can we call you Freder-Rico?" Krista asks.

...no...

"Oh, sorry. Well, what about Freddy?"

...yes...

I can't help myself, "Freddy like Nightmare on Elm St or Freddy like Freddy Mercury?" I almost can't get my voice above a whisper. Please don't be Nightmare Freddy, I can't reconcile that kind of spiritual encounter with the ghost I feel like I've gotten to know so far.

The loud pop of the soundbar below the TV startles me so badly I let out a shriek. I feel like my heart is going to explode, further taxed to race past its limit as the opening bars of Bohemian Rhapsody pour from the speakers... I scream, I scream like a little bitch, and my fingers shoot off the planchette.

"Oh, my God!" Krista and Jolie shout in unison. I don't even wait to be told. I grab the tequila bottle and take a guzzle for my screams and fuck words. I need way more liquid courage right now. Jolie and Krista still have their fingers on the planchette and their gazes locked on the soundbar.

My hair moves away from my right shoulder, and a gentle caress graces my cheek. The stroke of a finger over my lips. "Fuck," Jolie whispers. She's watching me as invisible fingers comb their way through my hair.

She goes for the tequila this time, but she can't take her eyes off me. Bumping the bottle, she nearly knocks it over. We all scramble toward the middle of the table, trying to save the liquor and limes. Bohemian Rhapsody continues to play through the speaker, and the walls of my living room begin to pulse. Books vibrate on my shelves. Jolie and Krista hold the neck of the tequila bottle, their eyes darting around the living room.

Shaking and covered in cold sweat, I turn my attention back to the spirit board. A silent scream stalled in my throat as I shakily point, trying to get my friends' attention. The planchette is moving completely on its own. Nobody is touching it. It jerks and circles around, spelling out a bloodcurdling message from beyond the grave... *I... n... e... e... d... y... o... u... W... i... l... l... o... w.*

Krista's hand shoots forward, and she flips the planchette off the table and then rushes over to the soundbar, hitting the power button. Once the music is silenced, everything else stops, too.

The walls are still, and only our panting breaths can be heard. For several minutes, nobody moves. I rub my hands through my hair, trying to recreate the sensations from before. I know he was touching me. Trying to convey a secret message only for me. His gentle contact, in contrast to the physical energy that radiated through the room.

"No, no— that can't be it?" I frantically pat around on the carpet looking for the planchette. I have to know. Need me? For what? What does he need?

"We have to get him back! We have to ask more questions!" My panicked voice sparking my friends into action. We all crawl around on the floor searching for the planchette.

"I got it!" Jolie holds it up triumphantly and rushes back to the coffee table to place it in the middle of the spirit board. "Now, what?" she looks between me and Krista.

"No more tequila, that's for damn sure." Krista joins Jolie and me back around the coffee table. The three of us slowly, gently, replace our fingers back on the little triangle.

There's a long pause as we glance between each other, uncertain how to start again. I swallow my fear and go for it.

"Freddy, what do you need?"

No response. No feeling of energy sizzling in the atmosphere. No sense of trepidation or celestial connection. I scrub the planchette around the board, trying to jump-start it. But he's gone.

Chapter 11
Beyond the Veil

Willow

Fuck! I cut my finger again; I'll have bandages on every tip at the rate I'm going. I'm too distracted and anxious to be using a knife, but the southern girl in me needed to make refreshments for this evening.

I patch up my abused fingertip, wash the knife, then carry on slicing vegetables, cheese, and smoked meat for the charcutier board. As I load the decorative tray, I try to ignore the fact that it's Edgar Alan Poe themed with skulls and ravens all over it. Maybe once all the food is loaded, it will cover the design. It's bad enough that Krista showed up with chocolate cupcakes decorated like little graves with candy tombstones; she just shrugged and asked what else she was supposed to bring to a séance.

"Tequila, not graveyard desserts," I say. My hands are shaking. I can't stop the spinning of my mind since the night we used the spirit board. I've changed my mind so many times that I don't know which way is up. Freddy has been on my mind incessantly. Is he really Humphrey? Are they separate supernatural beings? How do I help him? Why me? Do I want it to be me? Why does the name Freddy sound so hot?

He's been silent since my friends and I tried communicating with him, and it has me constantly wondering where he is and what he's up to. I have to admit I've missed him. The house has felt cold and lonely without his shenanigans. I've been scared a few times since he came to live with me, sure, but nothing bad has happened; he's been sweet—

"Yo, earth to Willow. Does that celery owe you money, girl?" Krista is standing behind me, her hand coming to pat my shoulder. I put down my knife and cover my eyes with my hand, putting pressure on my temples to ease my aching head.

"Tonight is going to be fine, you'll see. I got a good feeling about this, and you know I'm always right." I take a deep breath and focus on her reassuring words. Krista is always right.

Smoke and incense. Madame Ophelia makes her rounds, opening cabinets, drawers, the broom closet... she looks in every nook and cranny to cleanse the space. My house smells less like coffee and vanilla and more like her spiritualist shop now. We're all seated on the living room floor around my coffee table. Reminiscent of the night Krista, Jolie, and I used the spirit board. The night Freddy said he needed me.

Her dark purple velvet tablecloth now drapes over the small table, and pillows from my couch and bed are scattered on the floor. Candles have been placed along the other surfaces of the room, but they've been left unlit. Madame Ophelia said they were for later.

Crystals and stones engraved with protective sigils have been placed around the table, the smell of oil and herbs permeating the room. Krista's spirit board is spread out in the center with Humphrey standing guard.

Madame Ophelia gave us a crash course in what to expect. It was supposed to make us feel more comfortable, but just imagining all the possible outcomes for tonight has me even more on edge, if that is even possible. I wring my hands in my lap and try to focus on the nice things Freddy has done for me and how he deserves to find peace.

Madame Ophelia turns out all the lights and uses a flashlight to make her way back over to the coffee table, where Krista, Jolie, and I are already positioned. She settles herself in front of a large white candle. The strike of a match pierces the silence of my living room as she lights the candle and turns out the flashlight.

Taking a fortifying breath, she prepares herself for the rigorous tasks of spirit communication. The anxious energy in the room weighs on us like a collapsed ceiling. The Madame lifts her arms, beckoning Krista, Jolie, and me to join our hands with hers.

"We are peaceful seekers of the spirit realm. We banish all negative energy in this space. We banish all spirits who would seek to harm." She begins to hum for a few seconds, then continues. "We seek to communicate with the spirit attached to this bottle, to the spirit of Humphrey. Make yourself known to us; let us know you are here." She continues to hum and chant.

My hands are sweating. What if I can't keep holding on to Madame and Krista's hands? What if I break the protective circle, and then we all get possessed?

"Calm your energy, Willow. Take deep breaths and listen, or you will miss the spirit." Madame Ophelia squeezes my hand reassuringly. The light of the single candle dances in the darkness. I don't know if my eyes are playing tricks on me or if the flame is actually elongating. The crystal pendulums on the table begin to sway, slowly at first, almost undetectable, then building momentum. The suspended crystals move in concentric circles around each other.

Madame Ophelia continues to chant and hum. I don't know what's real and what's my adrenaline playing tricks on me. I feel heavy, like I'm under a stack of quilts, but cold at the same time. My breath comes in short, shallow pants, and I'm afraid I'm going to hyperventilate. I look over to Krista, wondering if she's feeling this, too. She looks calm and peaceful, her head swaying back and forth in time with Madame Ophelia's chanting. Jolie has her eyes closed, her head tilted back slightly; she almost looks like she's sleeping.

"Come to us, Humphrey spirit, tell us your message. We want to help you." Madame Ophelia stops chanting briefly; it looks as if she is concentrating, as if someone were whispering in her ear. She nods her head intermittently. Fucking shit, is she talking to him? My chest is tight, the back of my neck feels hot, and sweat collects on my brow. I don't know how much more of this I can take.

The darkness overhead recedes slightly. Krista and I lock eyes across the table, and then we both slowly shift our vision upward. Several small orbs of light float above the coffee table. They look like eerie bubbles of energy that could pop at any moment. I look back down at Madame Ophelia, who is smiling like she's been gossiping with an old friend.

I need to know what's happening. I'm close to hysterics, but everyone else looks so calm. I try to take some steadying breaths; maybe my anxious energy is fucking this up.

The pendulums pick up speed, and the planchette begins to vibrate on the spirit board. It skitters and scrapes in circles and jerky shifts until it can begin to spell out a message, *...H...e...l...l ...o...W...i...l...l...o...w.* Ffffffuuuuuuucccccccckkkkkkkkk, fuck! It spins again— *...M...y...W...i...l...l...o...w.*

A stroke up the back of my hand, then my arm... the feeling of a warm and gentle hand embracing my cheek. Then my hair is brushed over my shoulder, there's a comforting grip on the back of my neck, like a lover about to pull me in for a kiss. It's so serial; I lean into the comforting and gentle touch, something like familiarity, and the feeling that you're cared for and protected washes over me.

The hand leaves my face, and I feel its absence ache in the center of my chest. The candles around the room all begin to slowly grow a flame where they had previously been unlit, as if someone were walking through the room, lighting each one as they passed.

"Freddy?" I tentatively call out into the room. The planchette bobbles and then gently glides across the spirit board *...yes...*

"Why are you here?"

...t...r...a...p...p...e...d...

An overwhelming mix of sadness, bitterness, anger, and frustration courses through me. I feel slightly nauseated with the quick fluctuations in emotions; these aren't coming from me... these are *Freddy's*.

Madame Ophelia's head bobs around, and she's resumed her chanting. I worry that she is being overwhelmed by Freddy's emotions as well until she lifts her head up, illuminated by the candle's flame in front of her. Her face shifts, the features contorting, the softness of her full cheek becoming solid and angled, like she has two faces instead of one, both visual simultaneously. My jaw hangs open in disbelief. Is this Freddy? Or Humphrey? The features are obscured by the combination of his face merged with Madame Ophelia's. There's something recognizable, but not...

The planchette scrapes out a final message.

...n ...e ...e ...d ...y ...o ...u ...

The smell of extinguished wicks and melted wax lingers in the air. Madame Ophelia gently packs her crystals and pendulums into her bag. Krista is perched on my kitchen counter, stuffing her mouth full of graveyard cupcakes.

"Where do I go from here?" I approach Madame and offer her a glass of water. She smiles and thanks me for the drink. Taking the glass and gulping it down. I'm sure the energy expenditure of what she's done tonight is extreme. How can she look so content after this? I feel more confused than before we started.

"Your Freddy is no ordinary ghost, my darling. He isn't a person who has passed away and then transitioned to the spirit realm." I don't know how to make sense of that. How does one become a ghost without dying first?

She takes my hands in hers, looking deeply into my eyes with imploring tenderness. She says, "My darling, this is a very special opportunity the universe has brought to you. Consider the path you choose very carefully because this will change your life dramatically." She gives my cheek a gentle pat, then releases me.

Krista hops down from my kitchen counter and washes her cupcake down with a double of tequila. "So, Freddy's like stuck in that bottle, right?"

Madame Ophelia grins at Krista; they were instant friends when she arrived at my house this evening. "Yes, my love, sadly, he is tied to the vessel for eternity, it would seem."

Krista nods, her thinking face in full effect. "So, how does that happen? Like Willow, Jolie, and I have all handled Humphrey... are we gonna like poof into the bottle with him? Is it safe to have the bottle around?"

Madame Ophelia nods her head at Krista's concerns. I hadn't even considered that we were at risk of getting sucked into the bottle.

"This is a very special bottle, it resembles a witch's bottle, more specifically a bellarmine jug. These bottles were traditionally adorned with the face of a man, and the practitioner would fill the bottle with sharp items like nails, bits of hair, and such. It was typically used to draw out and capture negative energy. The spirit would be baited by the bits of hair or fabric belonging to the person it was tormenting, then once in the bottle, the spirit would be trapped by the sharp objects within." She takes another deep drink of her water.

"But I thought Freddy wasn't a bad ghost? Isn't that what we just learned?" I squeak.

She shakes her head yes as she swallows her water. "Yes, I said this bottle *resembles* a bellarmine, the face on the bottle, and the fact that you have a trapped spirit. But the base of this bottle is made of a special stone. It has properties of self-healing, connecting past lives, and physical and emotional healing. The bottle smells of herbs and oils typically used for finding love and expelling negativity. Unique indeed." She sets her glass down on the counter and lifts her heavy bag over her shoulder.

"My ride is here, my darlings." She heads to the door but turns back before she leaves. "Willow, you need to make a choice. Will you help Freddy find peace? Or..." She shrugs her shoulders, leaving the second half of the choice open-ended. "Remember, everything in this life and the next is connected. Sweet dreams, my lovelies." She blows us a kiss, and then she's gone.

After the slam of the door, Krista and I both turn to look at Humphrey, who is still sitting on the coffee table, grinning like a damn fool. The Madame never really answered our question about the risk of handling the bottle.

"Willow, just leave him there for now. We can figure out our next move in the morning. I think if he wanted to possess your soul and walk around in your body like a skin suit, he would have done it already." I turn my head to look at my friend. She's always been such a strong, no-nonsense, logical thinker. I need to channel my inner Krista to get me through the rest of the night.

"You're right. Let's clean up the kitchen, polish off this tequila, and crash." Krista hits the music streaming app through the TV, classic rock, her favorite station... but when Queen's "Another One Bites the Dust" is the first one on the queue, I snatch the remote back and change that shit to 90s Hip Hop. Krista, Jolie, and I burst into hysterical laughter because if I don't, I seriously might cry.

I'm blinking up at my dimly lit ceiling, lying next to Krista on my queen-sized bed. I don't normally need a nightlight, but tonight I just couldn't sleep in total darkness. Not that I'm sleeping. Jolie left after we got shit faced and cleaned up. There was no way her fiancé was letting her spend the night in my haunted house. I get it, but I'm glad to have Krista's company after tonight's antics.

The crescent moon nightlight with the suspended ambient star twinkles, slowly casting shadows on the room like the reflection of water in an aquarium. Fitting, because I feel like I'm drowning.

"I hear you thinking, bitch." She's always had that special gift; it means Jolie and I don't get away with shit, I just thank my lucky stars she's always used it for good and never evil.

"How do you do that?" I feel her shrug next to me.

"I dunno, it's not everyone I can sense shit with, just the people that matter most to me. Guess y'all are the only people that I care enough about to learn all your tells. Otherwise, I'd be knocking off casinos and living in a high roller penthouse." She snorts.

I try to sort my thoughts. There is so much to process. I have a ghost-man who lives in the Humphrey bottle, and he is trapped there by a... love spell? I don't know anything else about him, except that his name is Fredrick. And he likes to take care of others, or me at least.

That sounds really nice. I imagine having proper introductions: *Hi, I'm Fredrick, I like to take care of others, and hope to fall in love someday.* I'd shake his hand and say *I'm Willow, and I....* What would I say to a love-trapped ghost-man? *I'm Willow, and I'm a selfish bitch who just wants you to disappear so I can continue my lackluster life,* or *I'm Willow, I am a doer and a problem solver, I want to help you.*

"Feels like you just made up your mind." Krista yawns next to me.

I'm walking down a busy city street, but something isn't right. The signs and the way people are dressed don't feel right, but also seem like they belong. The logic is right at the tip of my brain, but I can't quite grasp onto it.

My feet are bare, I'm naked, and fearful of walking in public so exposed. The smell of sawdust fills my nose. I look around for someone, someone that I'm expecting, because I smell sawdust, but I don't know who I'm looking for.

I keep moving forward. The street is getting busier, and I feel overwhelmed by the crowd. They squeeze in close to me, too close. It makes me want to walk faster to get space between us, but no matter how hard I push myself, I can't gain any speed or distance.

I'm being herded by the crowd. The fabric of scratchy wool suits scrapes at my skin, women's handbags slap at me. They don't acknowledge me at all, not with looks, no one speaks. It's too quiet here, like the sound has been sucked out. Nothing, not shoes on the pavement, not the sound of breath as the man next to me huffs over my shoulder, the air from his mouth puffing my hair.

I'm herded to a shop door. The crowd at my back is relentless, and I'm pressed into the glass door so hard I'm afraid it's going to shatter and cut me to bits. My face smashes into the clammy surface, and I begin to panic and frantically push back against the crowd, but I can't move them an inch. My vision blurs, then focuses on the lettering on the shop door, just even with my nose... ODDITIES.

Finally, the crowd overtakes me, and the glass door shatters... I scream, but the sound is sucked out before it can break free...

I wake with a start, drenched in sweat and panting from my near-death dream. Krista sleeps peacefully beside me, undisturbed. I flop back down on my pillow and focus on my breathing. My heart is pounding so hard that it hurts. That was terrifying and bizarre. What the fuck does that even mean? It was so vivid that I felt like I was really there. My feet still have the lingering sensation of cold cobblestones on my bare skin, and the palms of my hands burn from being pressed against the glass of the shop door. Too much tequila and stress. My mind focuses on the lettering on the shop door: ***ODDITIES***. I am odd, aren't I? Always have been. I thought I was at peace with who I am, but maybe I was wrong.

I strain to hear any sounds from the front of the house. The gentle footsteps of Humphrey, no, Freddy, wandering the living room, would be a comfort right now. The eerie silence makes my skin crawl. Then the soft rhythmic tap comes from the living room toward my bedroom door. I breathe a sigh of relief knowing he's out there, watching over us.

CHAPTER 12
TICK, TOCK

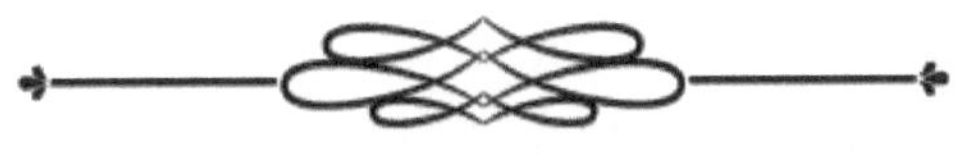

Gerald

FUCKING JUNKER. THE SQUEAL of the brakes is giving me away. This busted car I jacked sticks out like a sore thumb in this neighborhood. Not high class, but quaint. Smaller houses with flowers in the front yard, grass neatly cut. I bet every neighbor knows each other. They probably go to each other's houses for grills and holiday parties. Probably the kinda nosy bitches that call the cops when they see a strange car on their street. I shoulda jacked something nicer. My phone buzzes from the cup holder, the sound more jarring than it should be. But at this point, every vibration sounds like a gunshot to my ears.

Unknown: Tick tock, G

That text is like ice water down my spine. They've been coming steadily every day. Random times, but every day without fail. Fuck, I know I'm running outta time, he doesn't need to keep reminding me. The image he sent a few nights ago is seared into my mind. Ricky's lifeless body, bloodied from brass knuckles, and hanging by his arms from the ceiling of some dirty warehouse. A hand reaching from off-camera to hold Ricky's head up for the picture.

I'm next if I don't come up with something fast. One hit for every dollar owed. That was the text message. I won't end up like Ricky. I can't.

Turning my attention back to the quiet neighborhood, I get a brief feeling of nostalgia. The quiet, peacefulness of stability I had growing up. That I could have held onto, but— I shake that regret away. I'm so close to getting it all back. Then it'll be done with. Then I can get back to climbing the ladder like I deserve. The fuck ups won't matter anymore.

I hold the paper receipt from the estate sale between my sweaty fingers; the pencil marks smeared from the lines. Looking up the block, I see the address I'm here for. A little porch; neat, clean, no car in the driveway. Hanging plants line the porch roof, making it hard for me to tell if there are security cameras there. I need a closer look without drawing attention.

Putting the car in gear, I squeal around a few blocks and park. Far enough away for the closest neighbors not to link me to the junker. I slip my phone into my pocket and slip out into the street, leaving the car door cracked to avoid the noise of shutting it. I pretend to stretch while scanning the street for any onlookers before taking a stroll. Walking the block like I belong. Taking in little bits of detail about houses on the street. Who has a dog, who looks like they're home during regular work hours, whose windows have curtains open? I need to know who might peg me or not.

I slow my pace a few houses back before my target, trying to look natural. Just a guy on a walk. I take my time as I stroll past her house, lifting my chin for a better view. I strain to see if I can look through a window from the street. All the curtains look drawn, fuck. As I get closer, I veer off into the grass in front of her porch, bend down, and pretend to fix my shoelaces. I take the opportunity to get a better view of the house.

This could be easy; there is no fence gating off the backyard. I could go in through a back door... Maybe, I'm finally gonna catch a break. Slipping my phone from my pocket, I fake a phone call. Turning my shoulder toward the house, I click the camera button while I pretend to talk and scan the rest of the street. I'll study these tonight to make a better plan. My internet search on the coffee shop and a look through her socials gave me a rough idea about her schedule. I could come back early in the morning... I'll have plenty of time, and it'll still be dark out to disguise me. In and out. Easy peasy...

"You don't live in this neighborhood, honey."

Fuck.

I turn to see this old bag in a bathrobe and curlers, lighting up on the porch next door. How long has she been watching me? Not good. She's probably got a little set of binoculars she keeps next to the window to spy on anyone she can.

"Hey, good morning." I give a friendly wave and a charming smile. "I'm out trying to get a little exercise," I say as I pat my stomach for emphasis. "I needed a change of scenery from my neighborhood to keep it interesting, haha." I slip my phone back into my pocket, keeping my movements easy and casual. Tilting my head to turn the scarred side of my face away from her, I try giving her a relaxed smile.

"Do you smell that?" She sniffs a few times at the air. "Oh, I know what that is, it's *bullshit*." She pins me with her eyes.

Cigarette hanging from her lips, and she tightens the tie on her bathrobe menacingly.

"I know self-defense. I take a class down at the community center," she says.

I take a step back toward the sidewalk to show I'm no danger to her. I don't need her to give my description to the cops. I bet she has them on speed dial and knows all their first names and favorite flavor of cookie. "I'm sure you can kick ass, ma'am." I walk backwards a few steps. "But, taking a walk on a public sidewalk isn't a crime."

"*Crime*? Who said anything about *crime*?" She takes an exaggerated drag. "You gotta guilty conscience, sugar?"

Fuck this old bag. She's gonna ruin my whole plan with her meddling. "No ma'am, have a nice day." I start down the sidewalk and quicken my pace as I turn the block and double back to my car. Checking my watch, 8:15 a.m., not a good time.

10:30 a.m.; three days later

This time I took the bus to a nearby park and walked the rest of the way here. I slowly stroll down the sidewalk, noting any differences in the houses from when I was here before. There are fewer cars in driveways. That's a good sign, fewer people home that might notice me prowling around. As I approach the target, the old bag isn't anywhere to be seen. Hopefully, she's tucked into her couch watching a soap opera or something. Again, I stop in the grass of the front lawn and pretend to adjust my shoelaces.

"Funny how your shoe gets untied at the same house."

Fuck. Where did she come from, thin air?

"Yeah, I guess they only stay tied for so many steps." I turn to greet the old bag. "That's a lovely bathrobe." I nod at her. She's in the same get-up as last time, smoking her cigarette on the front porch. How's she get out here and light that cigarette so quickly?

"Thank you, it's real handy too. I learned how to strangle a man with the belt in my class down at the community center." She exhales a stream of cigarette smoke and looks me up and down. Fuck this is the second time she's assessed me. If she calls the cops, her description will be even better. I shake that worry away. As long as I get what I need first, 'cause getting busted will be nothing compared to him. Ricky's face comes to mind, making my stomach turn.

"That's good, you stay safe, ma'am." I turn on my best charm and then speed walk down the sidewalk. I need a new plan. My cell goes off in my pocket. I don't need to check, I know it's him. Cold sweat trickles down my back at the reminder.

Tick-tock

Tick-tock, tick-tock, tick-tock… the clock on the kitchen wall taunts me with the reminder of the threatening text messages he's been sending. I pace back and forth in front of my beat-up couch. What am I *gonna* fucking do? What am I *fucking* gonna do? I can't go strolling through that neighborhood again. "Old bag" will have made me for sure. I'm taking drags off my cigarette like it's my lifeline, I should slow down, can't even fucking afford to buy cigarettes at this point.

Tick-tock, tick-tock, tick-tock… the clock just keeps going. Why won't it shut up? It's never been this loud before. The ticking mocks me, mechanical laughter chastising me for all my past mistakes, punctuating the guilt of screwing over my family, the humiliation of all the lost bets. "SHUT! THE! FUCK! UP!" I scream as I rush into the kitchen and rip the fucker off the wall, smashing it onto the linoleum. I raise my foot and stomp on it over, and over, and over. I can't smash it enough to unhear the ticking. I just want to stop hearing the ticking.

Finally, when I'm panting and standing in the middle of shattered glass and plastic, there is a soothing blanket of silence— yes, silence, that's what I needed. A moment to breathe, regroup, to plan. I can do this. Soon, it'll all be settled, and I can start fresh. I can get it all back.

Pulling out my cell, I flip through the shitty pictures I got of the front of the house. They're mostly blurry, fucking worthless. I chuck the phone down and throw myself on the couch. It's stained with God knows what, and the springs stab into my back. Closing my eyes, I try to take some slow breaths. I can't plan when I'm all keyed up. I just need to calm down, relax for a minute, and then I'll come up with something. I have to come up with something.

The vibration against the surface of the coffee table breaks my short-lived peace. It's him, I know it. I scrub my hands over my face and fist them into my hair. Pulling hard on the roots, letting the pain override the fear that's icing my veins. I see Ricky again. Then I picture myself in that warehouse, my hands chained to the ceiling. Bile burns my throat at the thought. I shoot up from the couch and head back into the kitchen.

Bending down and shuffling my fingers through the debris, I find my cigarette. I pick off a piece of glass from the end. My hands tremble as I bring it to my lips and take another drag from what's left of the stub before heading back into the living room. The sensation I'm gonna vomit hits hard as I convince my hands to pick up the phone. I swipe the screen and find my messages. One new. This time there's no text in the message. It's a weblink. Fighting the urge to destroy the phone like I did the clock, I take a few ragged breaths and dig deep to find the balls to click on it...

A countdown. It's a fucking countdown. And when the time runs out, I'm a dead man.

CHAPTER 13
THE FOOL

Willow

I AM SO FUCKING stressed out! When I'm stressed, I get off. I can't get off with a ghost in my house?! He'll see everything. Fuck, fuckety fuck!! Okay, deep breaths, that is what I need. Think calming thoughts. Mrs. Graham said a man was casing my house... not creepy at all. He was probably just enjoying the neighborhood, as he said. Mrs. Graham can be extreme and quirky sometimes. I'm sure she is wrong. Although she wasn't wrong that time she said something terrible was going to happen, and then three days later, there was a twenty-car pileup on the freeway.

And there was that time she said she thought the Stanleys across the street were going to get divorced. I said there's no way 'cause I just saw them at the park and they seem like a perfect family. Then, like a month later, Mrs. Stanley found out Mr. Stanley was doing his secretary and threw all his shit on the front lawn and torched it. And what about that time she predicted that tornado that tore up the mall a few years ago...

I AM SO STRESSED OUT!!

Freddy could be anywhere. That is equally comforting and creepy. Comforting to think he is watching over me, and creepy to know he is watching me. Also, kinda hot to know he is watching me. I'm fucked in the head. I throw myself back onto the bed with a huff and stare at the ceiling. Why me? Why my life? Maybe I should have married one of those guys my mom tried to stick me with.

If I were in a stuffy mansion sorting my pants suits by color and getting lousy missionary from a small dick rich prick every night, I wouldn't be stressed the fuck out about some creeper casing my house right now, or the fact that I have a literal ghost tagging along everywhere I go. Who am I kidding? I would never make it in a stuffy mansion. I'm this girl, a 'lives with a literal ghost' girl. An 'every day I get more used to and into that I live with a ghost' girl. It's why I started carting Humphrey around everywhere again. I realized how lonely I was when I left him behind.

Like right now. There's a change of energy. I feel him. Humphrey. Freddy. I feel the shadowy presence in my room. What should logically be terrifying and chilling is comforting and homey. "Freddy, I know you're there," I call out into my bedroom. The feeling of a warm hand on my knee has me lifting my head to look at nothing. "Thanks," I say. It's an intimate and reassuring touch, one that says *I'm here for you.*

"That's nice of you, Freddy. Look, I'm sorry if I've been insensitive. This is my first experience with a paranormal roommate." I talk into the open bedroom space, trying to guess his face he might be, his hand now gone from my knee makes it more difficult. "I know you can't help being stuck to that bottle. I just happened to be the person who brought you home." I sigh in resignation as I remember that fateful afternoon. I always believed a person's energy lingered on their belongings, but this was more than I had anticipated.

Talking to "yourself" to someone, something, else can really make a girl feel crazy. But I continue anyway, "I wanted to tell you how much I appreciate you." I sit up on my elbows. "I'm willing to bet my life's savings that you are the nicest ghost roommate in world history. And don't think I haven't noticed you helping around the coffee shop and getting my coffee ready in the mornings." The pathetic truth of what I'm about to admit has my eyes tearing up. "You are the most thoughtful guy I've ever had in my life."

I crack, the tears win, and I start crying like a baby from all the shit that keeps piling on. The long work hours, my mom blowing up my phone about dates, being scared of a ghost, getting attached to said ghosts, and now a creeper in the neighborhood...

"I AM SO STRESSED OUT!" I squeeze my hands into fists and have a little mini tantrum on my bed. I'm getting ready to flop myself back dramatically onto my duvet when I get a smack to the face with something firm and rubbery. To my absolute horror, my alien unicorn vibrator is floating in midair, mouth level, and teasingly poking at the corner of my lips. *Nudge, nudge.*

"FREDDY!!!" I jerk back, aghast with the crude invitation. "You can't help yourself to other people's sex toys! That is very rude manners for a house guest, even if you are a ghost." The pink and blue tie-dye vibrator waggles in front of my face suggestively. I hold my breath as the tip moves closer to graze down my breast, bumping over my nipple, to trail its way toward my pussy. The tip slips under the hem of my cotton shorts, caressing my skin sweetly. It occurs to me that Freddy understands what I need.

I shoot up from the bed to stand in front of my floating sex toy and cover my face in mortification. I peek through my fingers, my gaze locked on the tip still pointing at me. How many times did I do this between buying the statue and realizing I was being haunted? Visualizations of my favorite toys, positions, and fantasies come flooding into my mind. Sitting on my bed, riding my Dracula dildo... the feeling of strong hands squeezing my breasts, holding my hips to grind me down onto the toy, how the orgasms have been so much better lately, the fantasies so much hotter... Holy shit, I fucked a ghost.

My mind reels; my naked body exposed to him, big titties, jiggly ass, the dirty things I say out loud, I said them to *him*. My breasts feel achy underneath my t-shirt with the memories of his touch. The bruises on my hips the next day. I fucked a ghost, and I did it over and over again. Oh my God!

"Freddy, um, uh, have we... have we, uh, you know..." I swallow the saliva coming up my throat. "Have we fucked, Freddy?" I whisper the question, losing my nerve. My answer is a sweep of the rubber cock head tenderly across my cheek and down my jawline. I fucked a ghost.

I am traumatized and also wickedly turned on. I can't argue with the amazing orgasms I've been "giving myself" lately; it's because I had help. *Gulp*. "Was it also good for you, hehe," Inappropriate, yes, but what else can I say? My head is going to explode, or maybe my vagina.

The dildo waves in front of my face, up and down, in a yes direction, oh wow. I fucked a ghost and he liked it. Any rational thoughts about what this means evaporate, replaced by intense desire. All my spookiest dreams come true. Before I can absolutely lose it, an invisible hand comes to the base of my skull, threading fingers into my hair and guiding me down to my knees. My unicorn alien cock traces my lips, I work up some saliva to lubricate it and open my mouth ready to receive. Gliding in, slowly at first. The phantom hand behind my head tightens its grip in my hair. The angle of the dildo shifts upward, causing my head to arch back, his pace increasing, until I'm gagging and saliva comes pouring down my chin. He pulls back for a brief moment, allowing me to catch my breath, hand leaving my hair, and the toy pulling out of my mouth.

Fingers brush the hem of my shorts and urgently dig their way under. The first graze to my clit has me shrieking in surprise. It morphs into a yearning moan as the toy slides back into my mouth. His fingers sliding through my pussy keep pace with the pump of the alien cock. Ahead of me, my reflection in the floor mirror of my bedroom is the image of a needy slut. Her hands gripping the life out of her knees as she writhes on the floor sucking giant alien cock, slobber on her chin, and a bulge between her legs to grind on.

It's the bulge in my shorts that I can't take my eyes off of. Leading in through the leg and into the crotch, I can make out the outline of his knuckles. My ghost's hand, fingering my pussy while he pumps my throat with a toy cock. Freddy's hand. Regret flushes me, regret that it's not Freddy's cock also. MMMMmmmm Freddy's cock... imagining the smell of his skin pressing on my nose, I get a phantom whiff of something woody and clean, like when you empty a pencil sharpener.

I slurp and hump until I'm so hot and needy, my tempo becomes erratic and I'm moaning around the toy that's stretching my lips and jaw. *Ahhh, ah. Ah. Ah. Ah. Ahhhhhaaaahhhh,mmmmmmmh-hhh*, my squeal is muffled by my full mouth. He pets me down, gently stroking over my clit as I continue to suck at the toy. Only when I pull away does he slowly slip his hand from my shorts.

The feeling of my hair being brushed from my sticky forehead and fingers sliding gently through the tresses of my locks follows. Tender caresses. I close my eyes and sigh. I melt into the floor, spread out on my fluffy rug, panting. After a moment, I feel gentle fingers pulling at me. This time it's the waistband of my shorts. I lift my hips as much as I can to be helpful. "It's okay, give me a minute and I can change my own clothes."

My shorts are pulled over my round ass and about halfway up my thighs before they are used to band my legs back up against my stomach. My pussy and ass are totally exposed, and my body folded in half. Seconds go by, nothing else happens. I lift my head off the floor and see for myself what's going on. In the mirror, I see a vulgar, raw image of my folded legs and slick, puffy pussy, wet and glistening with cum. I am completely spread open. A warm, wet sensation starts right at the base of my pussy and slithers up to circle clit. It spreads and presses against me. Slow savoring, I can see the movement of my pussy lips in the mirror as he licks against one side then the other, the swirl of my flesh as he circles his invisible tongue. That is hot as fuck.

"Freddy, oh," I whine and moan in a begging breath as he takes his time, cleaning my cum from what he already did to me. He presses and circles around my clit fervently, and I cum again quickly and harder. The image of my pussy pulsing against nothing in the mirror is an erotic mind trip, but I feel him, I feel his hot, wet mouth terrorizing me.

I'm struggling to catch my breath, legs still spread open in the air, when I hear urgent knocking on my front door. Freddy immediately releases me, the loss of him abrupt and irritating. I roll to my knees, and Freddy's hands are back helping straighten my clothes. The knocking persists. I fumble with my hair as I approach the door and look out of the peephole.

I turn the knob and pull open the door; it slams right back into place. I turn to see the lamp from my side table floating in the air, ready for a strike. "Freddy, it's just Krista, please put my lamp back." The second attempt to greet my friend goes much smoother. "Krista, what are you doing here?" I try to keep my voice upbeat and casual, totally not a 'I just got wrung out good and hard by my ghost man' voice.

"Bitch, I have been blowing up your phone for an hour. When you didn't answer, I decided I had to come straight over. You need to see this." She freezes mid-step en route to my coffee pot. "Why do you look and smell like sex, Willow?" Shit, super inconvenient time for Krista's best friend superpower, where she can tell all your secrets.

Ignoring her, I move to put on some coffee. She leans in close to me and takes a big sniff. "You got a man in here, Willow?" Krista begins looking around the living room suspiciously. Sniffing like a bloodhound, she follows a trail through my living room toward my bedroom, then U-turns back toward the living room. She stops in the center of the living room and takes a deep inhale.

"There's nobody here, Krista. Just the usual crowd. Me, you... and Freddy." I could slap myself for mentioning Freddy.

"OH MY GOD, DID YOU FUCK FREDDY? You spooky bitch, you did, didn't you?"

I hold my head in my hands. I can't meet her eyes. I don't even have my mind wrapped around this development; how can I explain it to her? "Krista, I…"

"Girl, get you some, our Freddy is a super hottie." She lifts my hand away from my face and high-fives herself, then slaps my ass as she scoots past me to grab a coffee pod. Dumbstruck, I become another appliance in my kitchen as she helps herself to coffee and creamer. "Aren't you gonna ask me how I know what your paranormal booty call looks like?" She asks over her shoulder.

Krista leans back against the kitchen counter and blows into her coffee mug, waggling her eyebrows at me. "Let me guess, Madame Ophelia has been tutoring you as a medium?" I ask.

"Nope," she moves back toward the living room where she had set down an old, yellowed newspaper on the side table. "Do you remember that I bought that box of old newspapers from the estate sale the day you got Humphrey?" She looks back at me expectantly.

"Yeah, you were going to make that custom coffee table with them, right?"

"Right," she lifts up the newspaper and waves it in my face. "I was sorting them out to organize the layout, and guess what I saw…" She flicks the paper at me.

Unfolding the page, I read the small headline. It's an article about a local carpenter who has gone missing. His foreman and coworkers petitioned the public for any information regarding his disappearance. There's a photograph of a group of carpenters gathered around a large worktable.

Pictured third from the left is a man named Fredrick Hughes. His foreman reported him missing after he neglected his shift three days in a row. Fredrick had never missed work before. After having no luck finding him at home, the foreman and coworkers pitched in to place an advertisement in the newspaper, hoping someone knew what had become of Fredrick.

I try to imagine what it must have been like for his coworkers to worry about him, never getting closure. Then I think about how Freddy must feel, being ripped from his life suddenly. Able to see and experience the passage of time with others but never being known himself. "Krista, we have to help him."

It hasn't rained in days, so why are there drips falling on my head from the awnings on this block? The rusty tin gutters are leaking God knows what in tiny dollops right in the center of my scalp. I walk with both hands over my head for protection. The neon hand of Madame Ophelia's shop glows in the window. I straighten my bag on my shoulder and pull the door handle.

Just like last time, I'm slammed with patchouli. The bookshelves lining the walls of the shop have been reorganized since my first visit. The Tarot tapestry on the opposite wall brings a shiver down my spine at the memories of our séance. From the back hallway, a beautiful and mysterious woman steps through the beaded fringe curtains. "I am Madame Ophelia. Welcome to my humble shop. I have been waiting for— oh, it's you. Well, hello, Willow *darling*."

Hm, so I guess she does say that to all the girls. Madame Ophelia is dressed in another boho-style skirt with quilt squares, this one in jewel tones. Her hair is down this time, her champagne curls flowing over her shoulders, a crochet-style scarf draped artfully around her neck. Her easy mannerisms and flowy aesthetic have a soothing effect.

"You've been expecting me?" I give her a skeptical look.

"Well, I did tell you to come visit me anytime," she says with a smile. I can't help but giggle at her sly expression. She knows damn well I can't sit on the sidelines of skepticism any longer. I'm not the same girl from our first meeting.

"Come on back, my lovely." She holds the beaded curtain open, welcoming me in.

We are seated on the floor on big fluffy cushions, incense smoke snakes through the air, and Madame Ophelia lights candles, illuminating metal hanging lanterns. She hhmms softly to herself as she uses practiced fingers to shuffle her deck. "Let's pull a card before we begin shall we, just for fun." She smiles warmly at me as the deck ripples in her hands.

Offering me the deck to cut, she gestures gracefully with her upturned palm, "Please, draw a card, my love." I close my eyes and try to feel which card calls to me. Gently pulling one out with my index finger. Madame takes it from me and sets it aside. "For later, yes?" She pats my hand reassuringly, then reaches for the tea tray to pour us each a cup.

I swear she puts weed in this tea. I feel so fucking calm when I drink it. We sit in peaceful silence for a few moments, 'resting in the space', as she puts it.

"I see you have brought a guest with you today?" She motions toward my bag. Humphrey. I pull him out and plunk him down between us. He grins like a kid on Christmas. His smiling face hides all the answers I need.

"I felt it was only fair to include him in this conversation," I say, taking a deep breath. "The night of the séance, he said he needed me. I didn't understand at first. I was stuck in my mind. He was a ghost, a poltergeist. What could he need me for?" Madame Ophelia patiently nods along as I unload my feelings. "But, you said he was more than that. And then Krista found this old newspaper." I take the paper from my bag and unfold it to show her. "See, there he is. That's Freddy. He just vanished, and his friends were looking for him, but he's been trapped here. I need to help him, but I don't know where to start." I huff into my tea cup.

"How do you set a ghost free from a charmed object? Is that even possible? Can I help him cross over?" My eyes burn with tears, and I imagine how lonely and heartbreaking his existence has been these decades alone with the bottle.

"I can't let him suffer anymore." My voice cracks with emotion for Freddy. He's become like a friend to me, more than a friend. I've grown so used to his energy in my space now, I know I'll be heartbroken when he's gone. We've shared some intimate moments. Not just sexual ones. He's held me every night because I've been scared of the creeper man. He tucks me in a blanket when I fall asleep reading and makes sure my bookmark goes in the right place.

Madame Ophelia holds her hands out to me, beckoning me to place my palms on hers. She draws several deep breaths, lolling her head back as she seeks whatever information she can find. Time feels frozen; the silence sucking me into a feeling of limbo. The only sounds in the room are our breathing and the occasional spark from one of the hanging lanterns. When Madam finally opens her eyes, she nods in agreement, as if she's having a private conversation. I wait respectfully to hear her words.

"You have a journey ahead, Willow. Be discerning. Not only so you make smart choices, but also that you listen closely to your heart. I agree, you are an important piece in his path to freedom. However, there are many roads that can lead to the same result. Choose wisely." She releases my hands and waves over the Tarot card I pulled earlier. I shoot my hand out to stop her.

"Why me? Why would the universe pick me? What could possibly be gained by making him wait literally decades for some random girl to find him at an estate sale?" I can't make sense of why, why of all the people in all the time he's been trapped, did it have to be me?

"The universe is wild and unruly, Willow. We cannot tame it into logical details. Sometimes it takes longer to learn our lessons," she pats my hand and reaches for the Tarot card again.

"Let's see what message is for you today, yes?"

My hand feels weighted down with cement as I reach for the card and flip it over.

"Ah, The Fool." She lifts her hands in appreciation for the drawn card. "The Fool is for new beginnings, journeys, or maybe an awakening. It calls us to step out of what is known and into what is unknown, but also cautions us not to be hasty."

I feel foolish for sure. I have answers now, but I still feel lost. I stare down at the Tarot card, lost in my swirling thoughts. Madame Ophelia drapes something around my neck. Touching the stone in the center, she says, "Moonstone, to help guide you, my love."

CHAPTER 14

HUMPHREY

Fredrick

JACK. JACK LOOKED FOR me. Part of the devastation of bleak eternity in isolation is the thought that your mortal life wasn't much different. No one to share your accomplishments and failures with. I'm sure my disappearance was convenient for Isabelle.

Knowing that even though it was fruitless, an effort was made on my behalf... it eases some of the grief. I smooth my hand over the aged print, my past life staring back at me from the photograph. Surreal. How am I still that man? I feel like I haven't changed in decades, stagnant, and yet I feel so detached from that man, do I even know him anymore?

Willow sits on the living room floor with her laptop, searching for information on Tarot readings and witchcraft. I study the beauty of her face in the electric glow. Madame Ophelia was right to say our paths are intertwined. I felt celestially connected to Willow from the very moment she entered Edith's home.

I lie to myself that this connection is about celestial bonds between soulmates. That fate somehow brought us together across time and space. The more likely reality is that she will discover how

I am to pass on. Fickle am I. Wanting that very thing all these years, and now...

Reaching out, I gently glide my fingers through her silky golden strands. Fingering the tips, reluctant to release them. Her eyes drift closed briefly, and a smile hints at her face. She closes her laptop and turns her face in the direction she assumes me to be. She waits a beat, then sets the laptop aside and pulls the spirit board out into the middle of the floor. With shaking hands, she places the planchette in the middle and whispers, "Freddy? Can you move that by yourself?"

Hovering my hand over the planchette, I gently coax it toward yes. Willow doesn't move; I don't even think she's breathing. It's taking tremendous courage for her to face me head-on. It's one thing to lose yourself in a fantasy of desire, another to speak directly to the ghosts that haunt us.

She musters herself with a glassy-eyed expression then asks again, "Freddy, how did you get in the bottle?"

The question slices my chest as the memories flood back. Questions and decisions that have followed me around for decades, but I can't make sense of them, no matter how much time passes.

E...D...I...T...H...

The planchette scrapes along the board, spelling the only clue I really have because the truth is, after all these years, I still don't fully know. Except that I've only myself to blame.

August 1939, London

I kick a small stone with the toe of my leather boot as I trudge down the street, my hands jammed in my pockets, and my shoulders hunched. I fiddle with the diamond ring in the right pocket of my trousers. I slip it on and off the tip of my index finger. I should be slipping it on the reserved finger of Isabelle Kingston's left hand. Fate had other plans, though. It was a mistake to dream of a future with her. Her family was so much wealthier than mine- well, if I had one. Why would she marry an orphan and a carpenter? I dared to hope it was real affection and not just a pastime for her. I was wrong.

She laughed at me. Laughed at the small size of the ring, one of the few things of my mother's that I still have, and laughed at the idea of a proposal. Then told me she couldn't possibly marry me when she was already engaged to some stuffed pillock of a businessman (my words, not hers, although accurate). My dreams of the future floated away with the sound of her condescending laughter in the wind. I've been played a fool. I guess I can understand; she'd want as much security as she can get from marrying well, with the war and all.

I'm not even sure how far I've wandered, walking the streets of London until my chest aches less. I look to my right at the large advertisement, "You'd Feel Better if You had a Guinness," I'll say. The sign is posted above the hairdresser and the smoke shop. I've wandered into the little shopping district. I didn't mean to walk down this far, but I can't imagine going home to my small apartment to sit in silence by myself. I don't need a haircut, and I don't smoke. The next shop will do, Edith's Oddities: Collections from Around the World. Perhaps the strange shop goods will raise my spirits.

The chime on the door jingles as I enter, and wood panels creak beneath my feet. The air smells musty and a bit sour. This is a cramped little place with items stuck in every available nook and cranny. I think that is a necklace made of human teeth... There are candles and incense lined up in the glass cabinets. Maybe the shop owner should burn some to cover the smell of age and mildew. There are all manner of items everywhere you look. A bowl of skeleton keys, glass trays, old mirrors, large vases, African pottery, and little polished wood carvings of exotic animals.

I can barely squeeze between the shelves to walk around; there are items everywhere. I look to my left and come nose to snout with a giant mounted boar's head. Quickly, I turn the corner to the next aisle, just barely nicking the shelf and almost toppling a little statue. I fumble, but I'm able to catch it before it hits the floor. No telling what this would cost if I'd broken it.

A lady's voice comes over my shoulder, "Oh, good catch. That's a very special artifact indeed." In my hands is a statue of a little man dressed all in red sitting on a heavy stone base. She continues, "It's said that anyone who drinks from the bottle will mend what ails them." I look down at the statue again and notice the hat is actually a little stopper.

"That's a lovely thought, isn't it?" I respond, "That you could be healed of any affliction." When I turn back to face her, she's moved on. The shelves are so high I can't see where she's gone off to. I lift the bottle to set it back on the shelf and notice a sloshing sound that I hadn't detected before. Picking the bottle back up, it's much heavier now than a minute ago. Curious, I give it a shake. The sloshing is obvious; how had I not noticed before that the bottle was full? I uncork the hat stopper and look inside to see a dark liquid. Hmmm, smells like brandy.

A cure for what ails you, she said. I wonder can it heal a broken heart? I look around again to make sure the shopkeeper isn't watching. Lifting up the bottle, I take a giant swig of the dark liquid, and then everything goes black.

Willow's shocked gasp brings me back into the moment. "Edith?" she breathes. Her face grows pale, and she looks like she may vomit. "Did she... murder you, Freddy?"

...No...

"Then she cursed you?" she questions.

...No...

At least, I don't think she did. Edith did entice me toward the bottle, but I think it was more as a selling point for her shop than to coerce me into a curse. She's always expressed interest in the caretaking of the statue. If she cursed me, what would have been the reason?

I push against the planchette again. *H... E... R...* pause, *S... H... O... P* pause, *D... R... A... N... K...* pause, *H...U... M... P... H... R... E... Y...*

"You drank Humphrey?" Willow rises onto her knees and scoots over to the coffee table, where the little demon is watching us. She gingerly lifts him and gives him a little jiggle, then cautiously opens the cork and peeks inside. Unsurprisingly to me, he is empty. He's been empty every day since. Feeling a little braver, she tips him upside down and gives him a few hard shakes. The movement of the planchette draws her eyes back to me and the spirit board.

A... L...W... A... Y... S pause, *E... M... P... T... Y*

"Then what did you drink? Air?" She wrinkles her sweet nose in confusion, then quickly jams the cork back, setting Humphrey roughly down on the coffee table with a clank. He goes teetering around before landing on his side. "Oh, shit, I'm sorry! There's no telling what could happen to you if he gets broken!" she exclaims as she rights him.

M... A... Y... B... E... pause, P... A... S... S... O... N...

"Maybe pass on? You don't really know what your fate is, do you, Freddy?" She holds Humphrey more tenderly now as she contemplates my predicament. "Do you want to pass on?"

That question. I think I know the answer until I don't. Long, exhausting years, isolation, heartache, delusion... life just beyond the brush of your fingertips, both wishing for and fearing death. Was it death I longed for, or was it just an end to my suffering?

I swirl the planchette, unsure how to answer her. Before I can choose what to say, she asks, "Freddy, are you even dead?"

Am I even fucking *dead*? It had never occurred to me that I wasn't actually dead. Even if I hadn't been at first, after all these years?

I pace the aisle of the library while Willow pulls books from the shelves. I tried carrying the load for her, but was quickly rebuffed for causing a paranormal stir when the old librarian rounded the corner and nearly had a heart attack. Thankfully, Willow was able to convince her she was seeing things and maybe should go home and rest.

Now I have to stand back and watch her struggle under the weight of them. I wrap my arms around her from behind, placing my hands underneath the books to help lift them in her arms. Doesn't hurt that this position also affords me the luxury of Willow snuggled to my chest. Walking behind her like this makes my cock ache, my hips pressed into her plump ass, precum teasing the head of my cock as she bends forward to lay her books on the large desk.

I picture dripping my cum down the crack of her ass. I pull the heavy wooden chair back for her and slide in underneath so she's on my lap. "I can feel you, Freddy," she grits out. She can't make too big a fuss or the other patrons will think she's a nutter. In answer, I squeeze my arms around her waist and lift and roll my hips into her ass. I know she can feel the ridge of my cock snugged between her ass cheeks. Her little stifled gasp rewards me.

"We are here on official Humphrey business." Her eyes dart around, trying to discern who could be listening to her talk to herself. I should behave. I should. But... if I do pass on... I want to go on knowing I never wasted a second with her.

She dutifully tries to flip through the book; she's been spending all her free time searching for answers to my predicament. I should reward her efforts, shouldn't I? I slip my hands under the hem of her sweater, smoothing them over her stomach and pushing my thumbs under the bottom edge of her bra to caress the underside of her breasts. Her breath picks up pace. Her hands grip the edges of a book on the history of witchcraft. Her fingertips blanched from her efforts.

I work my right hand into the cup of her bra and squeeze her large, pillowy breast while I band her down with my left hand and roll my cock against her again. *"Ahhhh,"* she groans, met with a *"shhhh,"* from somewhere off to the side.

I wish I could see the blush that must be on her cheeks right now. Pushing my face into her neck, I lick up her pulse and nip at her earlobe. Can she sit here quietly like a good little library patron? Will she cum so loud that she's barred for life?

My mouth spreads in a wicked grin at the mental image. Sweet Willow, kicked out of the local library for public indecency... I run my left hand down under her waistband and into her knickers. She's already wet, slippery under my fingers. I glide between the lips of her pussy, softly caressing her sensitive nub. Squishing around in her lace knickers, being naughty in public, it turns her on. Who am I to deny my sweetling her dirty desires?

I can do better, though. I can have her dripping, fuck, I want her pussy to puddle in my hand. I thrust three fingers into her, spearing her and forcing her thighs wider. The wooden chair scrapes on the floor, causing several heads to turn in our direction again. She's trying so hard to play it off, patrons looking over their shoulders. They're wondering what she's up to. Willow tries to hide her face behind her book.

"Let them stare. Can they guess you're riding the fingers of a ghost until you're pouring out of your pussy with sweet honey nectar? Jealous gawking. Disapproving glances. They don't know how hot your cunt feels, how your pussy squeezes my fingers, the sinfully sticky slickness of you squelching around my hand." I curl my fingers in and press hard on that sweet little spot deep inside of her.

She wiggles and grunts (tries to play it off as a cough). "Nobody is buying it, my love. They see the depravity of our public spectacle. They see you rocking your hips ever so slightly into your chair. They see you bracing your forearms on the desk and hugging that reference book for dear life."

Her breath stutters and pitches, her efforts to be silent failing miserably. I feel it in her body before I feel it on my hand. The shudder, the tension, the locking of muscles in ecstasy. Then the rush of sticky, slimy, cum. It pools around my hand. Her pussy contorting around my fingers in a rhythmic pulse, *woosh, woosh, woosh,* hard and tempoed with the release of her fluids.

Her thighs are coated, her pussy drowning, my fingers immersed. "This is heaven. My woman under my fingers, seated on my lap, her breast in one hand, making delicious puddles in my other. Dripping for me."

All eyes are on her. Some filled with scandal, most filled with jealousy. My eyes, though, mine are filled with adoration.

I smirk with satisfaction as I follow Willow out of the library. Her ass swaying with her jacket wrapped tightly around her hips to hide the wet spot on the back of her leggings. Even if Humphrey wasn't stowed away in her backpack, I would follow her anywhere.

We left the library empty-handed. Even using Madame Ophelia's observations as a jumping-off point, we've made no significant gains in understanding. Humphrey seems to be a mixture of different spiritual tools like sweet jars, witch's bottles, and face jugs. Vessels where the ingredients housed within can aid in love, financial gain, or protection. But he doesn't quite fit any of them either. He is something altogether unique.

Our heads are swimming with teasing bits of information, but no definitive understanding. I should be frustrated, but I find that I'm happy. One day no closer to the truth means one day more with my Willow.

I stop suddenly as we approach her car. Something familiar and unsettling tickles my neck. I turn and search the block, but I don't see anything. She buckles Humphrey into the backseat like a toddler, and I slip into the front passenger side as she cranks the ignition. The sandy brick of the library shifts in my view, and I catch a glimpse of a figure just as it pulls back into the alleyway. Not a good enough look to make out their face, but again, I have the foreboding sensation of something ugly but familiar.

Lying on the couch, I hold Willow wrapped in my arms. Stroking the soft whisps of her hair while we listen to the rain. She was frustrated after the library research turned up a dead end. I wish she would rest her mind, but I can feel her wheels turning at top speed, even as we lie lazily together. "Don't you think it's strange that I can't find anything other than that sparse obituary?" She asks.

Willow rolls off the couch and scrambles over the carpet back to her laptop, her fingers a frenzy on the keyboard. She frantically opens tabs and types Edith Grant, Fayetteville, Arkansas. After several hours of searching, Willow lets out a frustrated groan.

Nothing. That is what she's found. Nothing regarding the death of Edith Grant. No local newspaper articles, no social media posts from close friends or extended family. It's as if Edith evaporated, like I did all those years ago.

"Maybe I need to go back farther into her life?" she muses to herself as she scrolls through unproductive search results. I reach for the planchette and spell out London. "London? That's really far back, but I guess that's the part where you two would have crossed paths. Good call, babe." Babe, the warmth of her endearment aches in my heart. More and more, I find myself dreading the day we solve the Humphrey mystery.

Clicking of keys in a stunted rhythm plays the soundtrack of our investigation. I lean over her shoulder as she scours old photographs of shopping districts in London that were associated with Edith's family name. This appears to be another fruitless trail until— I jolt forward to stop her from swiping the mouse pad.

"What is it?" She scans the screen of grainy images from old newspapers and photographs until I feel her body go tight. I know she sees it too. Edith's Oddities. The little shop door, deep set in the building's brick front, looks back at us from the electronic glow of the laptop screen. Painted lettering chipped, but still legible.

"I know this place..." Willow trails off. How could she possibly? Edith closed the shop shortly after I vanished. The war was looming closer. I remember her gentle whispers of encouragement to all of the wares as she packed us away, carefully wrapped in newspapers and old cloth.

Willow's face now pale, she closes the laptop and retreats to her room.

Chapter 15

Dreams

Willow

THE MEMORY OF A dream I can't shake; well, two dreams. Dreams I thought were unrelated until now. One so real that it awakened yearning within me. Something familiar that's been resting in the back of my mind. I recognized him immediately when Krista brought over the newspaper article. I didn't need to read the caption to know which man in the photo was Fredrick Hughes.

I've seen his face, his sweat-slicked body. I've felt his strong arms under my palms. Smelled him, tasted him. It was so real; I still sensed the taste of his mouth when I woke up, and the smell of sawdust. I can smell it now as I drift back to the memory of the dream, the fresh, sharp scent of earthy musk.

Desire, *more than desire*, connection, and the familiarity of a long-time lover pumped through my veins. Mine. The word rings in my mind. It feels so right, so familiar, but how? How can I feel so connected to someone from the past? Someone I've never met?

But that isn't true, is it? I do know Freddy. We've spent every day together for the last 4 months. Whether I knew it or not. He's been there for me when I was tired, sad, hungover, overwhelmed... It's too much to process fully. I don't understand what this means or how it's all possible.

The other dream is like a shock of ice water over my head. I feel queasy at the thought. A nightmare, the relief I felt when I woke up from the chaos of being crushed into a glass door by a mob. Fear of being shattered to bits and screaming without avail.

I stop pacing and fling myself onto the bed. How many times have I lain here in the last 4 months, staring at my ceiling, looking for the answers? Since I brought Humphrey home, I have been terrified of, comforted by, lusted for... Freddy... even before Krista brought that newspaper over. But it runs so much deeper than that now, and I don't know what to do with these feelings.

Are they real? Authentic? Are they the combined product of my wishful thinking, self-deprecation, and reality avoidance? Has the ingrained toxicity that I'm never going to have a normal re-lationship finally melted my brain, and now I'm insane? Having premonitory dreams about a man decades old, who happens to be haunting you, definitely fits the bill for a descent into madness.

Mental breakdown or not, I want him. I want the man from my dream. I want to see him, feel him, smell him. I want Freddy. I need Freddy. What if I never discover a way to free him? Even scarier, what if I do? What if he passes on and I never see him again? I have asked myself those questions on repeat.

The idea of an empty Humphrey, or an empty house, and an empty life without Freddy, has tears forming behind my eyelids. I scrunch my fingers into my hair and press the heel of my palms into my eyes, trying to press the sadness away. And would he feel the same? Would he choose to stay if eternal peace were the trade-off? Would he also feel like his heart is being ripped out of his body at the thought of leaving me behind? How can I ask him to make a choice like that?

A hand wraps around my neck, tender but firm. Holding me in place. My eyes drift closed, and I try to picture the man, solid and real, hovering over me. Fingers trace down toward my collarbone and continue to the tops of my breasts. The tears I've been trying to hold back trickle down my temples into my hair. The sensation of a finger traces their path. I blink the rest away, my eyes searching the empty air above me for the face I've seen in my subconscious. "Freddy," I breathe.

Warmth washes over me, like the hug of a lover. How I wish he were a solid entity, one I could hold, caress, feel... I am so fucked in the head that I'm falling for a ghost.

A puff of air trickles over my breasts like hot breath. Then he's gone. And I feel so empty. Lonely. With tearful eyes, I scan the room for any sign of him. Quickly wiping my eyes, I try to hide what I'm really feeling. He can't help it that he's a ghost. It's not his responsibility to cater to my irrational emotional attachment to him. I don't want him to feel guilty about wanting to pass on.

The bedroom is thrust into darkness. I panic at first, thinking the power has gone out, or is it the creep that's been stalking around my house? Rising on my elbows, I wait for my eyes to adjust. The stark darkness is eased into a golden hue as candles start to light on every surface; the ambient glow rises around me as flames flicker on my dresser, nightstand, and window seal.

A slow tempo from the soundbar in the living room floats into the space with the opening chords of "Wedding Song" by the Yeah Yeah Yeah's. The romantic atmosphere is overwhelming, and my lungs constrict with the intense emotions I'm feeling. Standing in my bedroom, in the luminous glow of tea light candles, a new tear trickles down my face. No sooner does the river crest the apple of my right cheek, a ghost of lips is there to catch it. Warmth envelopes me again, and I'm dancing with Freddy.

Pulled toward his body, the feeling of a face buried into my neck and hands in my hair, I clutch-n-sway with my arms wrapped tightly around a man I can feel as real as if he were standing here, but I cannot see. Hands slip under my t-shirt and find the edge of my bra, lifting my clothing over my head to be discarded on the rug. I can feel him, so vividly, his warmth against my bare breasts, so familiar. Just like my dream, as if this has happened a hundred times. We fit. We belong.

My panties are next, his hand slipping beneath the waistband at my back and over the curve of my ass cheeks as he peels them down my ass and thighs. It's too much to feel him and not see him. I have to close my eyes and forget that he isn't really here. I picture him, the man in my mind's eye.

His face, trailing down my stomach, follows my panties in descent. Pausing at my pussy, his tongue slides between my pussy lips, wet and soft. Gently exploring me. His hands gripping my ass, lifting my cheek up, and spreading them open. I feel the firm grip of his fingertips digging into my skin.

"Oh, my God, fuck! Fuck, Freddy, I feel you. I feel you everywhere!"

He sucks at my clit, my juices dripping between my thighs. My hands find his forearms that are wrapped around my hips and trace my way to his head. I can feel my fingers slipping through his thick, wavy hair; it's the softest thing I've ever touched. Holding his head

while he kneels in front of me and devours my sticky, wet pussy...
It's so erotic and intimate.

My legs are swept over his shoulders. In my mirror's reflection,
I see myself, naked, my hands gripping the invisible hair between
my thighs, as he grips my ass in his strong hands and writhes me
against his mouth. My body undulates in the mirror, feet dangling
above the ground. I'm levitated, but I've never felt more secure in
my life.

Vibration hums against my pussy, and I'm lifted further from
the ground, then carefully tossed onto my bed, my legs were forced
open as wide as possible. One of the candles from my dresser hovers
over my body, tilting slightly, allowing hot wax to drip over my
thighs and mound. The cooled wax flicked from my skin, then
Freddy's smooth tongue traces the path. Wax drips over my belly
and breasts. The sharp burning sting quickly dissipates with the
soothing comfort of his tongue laving over my flesh. It's like a
declaration. No matter what pain reality can bring, he'll be there
to soothe me.

His body presses over mine. I can feel the weight of him, his hard
to my soft. The pressure of his body weighing down on mine is
surreal when I cannot see him. The head of his cock brushes my
thighs. In all our interludes, he's never entered me. But I've had
his fingers and his tongue, why couldn't I have that too?

"Freddy, please..." he answers my incomplete plea with a smol-
dering kiss. His knee shifts to push my thigh further upward,
opening me up for him, then easily slides into me. The feel of his
hard cock stretching me open pulls a groan of pleasure from my
lips. I lift my head to look down my body. Visually, it would seem
I'm alone on my bed, but his girth is gliding steadily through me,

ramming my G-spot with hard, determined thrusts. I feel it, rising in me, the orgasm cresting. I arch my back into him, pressing my breasts into his chest, my nipples flush against him, I try to wrap myself as tightly as around him as possible. I'm shunted up the bed with the effort of his thrusts, my hair caught under my shoulders, holding my head back, exposing my neck for his mouth.

I'm consumed by him. The image in my mind's eye of the man from my dream, the man from the newspaper. Fredrick, my man, my ghost. The bloom of orgasm waves across my body, and I cry out, his name hoarse on my breath. "Fredrick!!"

"Yes, sweetheart, cum for me." I hear it, a whisper in my mind. Was it really his voice? Did I finally hear him? Or am I so lost for my ghost that I conjured his whispered words?

Morning light streams through the crack of my curtain. I turn my face away and into the warmth of the body next to me, holding me tenderly, under the blankets. Freddy's arm is draped over my waist, and his morning wood is pressed into my thigh.

I daydream of a life like this. Could I spend the rest of my days loving a man I could never see? Is that a deal breaker for a relationship? To the world, I'd look like a spinster, an old maid, forever single. But I'd have Freddy. How long would he want me? What happens as I grow older?

He's lived for decades, maintaining his youth. Based on his photo in the newspaper and my dream, I'd guess he was in his early thirties. But now he would be over one hundred years old. But I will continue to age. How long before I'm too old to hold his attention? What if I die and leave him behind?

I shake my head and will the negative thoughts away. I want him. For now, I just want to enjoy the happiness and sense of fulfillment I have with him. His form stirs around me, on the cusp of waking. My mind drifts to our quest. Searching for the answers about Humphrey and Fredrick's destiny. I feel like Edith is a key piece, but what happened to her? The most logical explanation is that she's dead...

My phone starts buzzing on the nightstand, the ringing unfamiliar. All my friends have dedicated music saved to their numbers. Stretching out my fingers, I scoot it closer toward me across the nightstand. I fumble, and it falls to the floor. Draping myself over the mattress's edge, I flip the phone over to view the screen.

No one is calling. It's the alert that the alarm system at Dripping has been tripped! "Oh shit!" Tossing the phone on the bed, I scurry around, getting dressed as quickly as possible. I don't even know what I'm throwing on.

I need to get to the coffee shop as quickly as I can to see what's happened. Most shops on the block are closed today, so there probably wouldn't be a witness if someone broke a window. What if a car drove through the front of the shop? What if someone broke in? Stopping to take a centering breath, I tell myself it's probably nothing, maybe the alarm tripped itself, or a bird flew into a window. Rushing through my living room, I snatch up keys and my bag and sprint out to my car.

I peel into the back parking area of my shop like a NASCAR driver. Racing up to the back door, I skid to a stop. The lock has been popped open, and the back door is ajar. Using my toe, I give the door a little push. Cautiously entering the shop, I flip my keys between my fingers like a makeshift weapon as I take a step over the threshold.

Smoothing my hand over the inner doorframe, I flip the light switch and listen. When I hear nothing, I venture a little deeper inside. Expecting to see chaos considering the state of the back door, I'm shocked to see that nothing looks disturbed. Tables and chairs sit neatly in the main area. The register and the front display cabinets are intact. There's no cash left here overnight, so I don't have to worry about them stealing the shop's earnings, but there's plenty of damage that could be done. A busted register or broken display glass would still be very expensive to fix.

Glancing around, it looks like there isn't anyone inside. The alarm is still singing; maybe they got spooked when it set off. I pull out my phone and call the local police to report the break-in attempt. While I wait for them, I try to look through everything as best I can without disturbing it, just in case. This is a safe area of the city. Nothing like this ever happens on the block. I hope none of the other shops were hit...

My hands are cramping from all the scrubbing, and my fingers have gone all pruney. After the police left, I went straight to the hardware store to change the lock. Then I got to work inside. I can't stop cleaning. I have been sanitizing and resanitizing the coffee shop for hours now. I feel violated. Someone was wandering around in here doing who knows what. What if they spit in the coffee carafes? Or sat bare-assed on the counter?

Knocking sounds from the front of the shop. Brushing my hands down my jeans, I walk from the back to take a look and see an older lady standing at the front door. Relieved that it isn't my burglar coming back for a round two, I flip the lock and open the door slightly. I'm still uneasy from finding my place broken into, and you can never be too careful.

"Oh, good, someone is here," she smiles at me. "I was hoping you were open when I saw the lights were on." She smiles sweetly.

"Actually, I'm not open today, I was working on my back door," I cringe at my own word choice, but hopefully she won't notice. "You know what?" I change my mind. "I was just about to make myself a cup. Why don't you come in and have one with me, on the house?"

"Oh, you are too kind, thank you so much. You know, sometimes I think coffee is what runs through my veins." She chuckles as she comes inside and takes a seat in one of the cushy booths.

"What can I make you?" I ask over my shoulder as I head to the sink to wash my hands.

"Oh, nothing fancy, honey, just good ole coffee with cream and sugar."

Dorthia is my new friend. She's a fan of classic horror movies, a coffee connoisseur, and is vice president of the local chapter of the Rose Society. Dorthia talks a lot. I don't mind, though. Her endless stream of conversation is what I needed after this morning's events. She was ready to suit up and ride when I told her about my incident. She has no patience for "*no-good thugs.*" Her phone buzzes a few times in her purse, but she doesn't seem to notice. "Dorthia, is someone trying to reach you?" I ask.

"Oh, my goodness. Thank you, honey. I never hear this thing going off. It's just my *lover*. He likes to keep track of me." She fishes her phone from her purse and sends a response.

"Your *lover*? Is he not your boyfriend? That sounds scandalous, Dorthia." I can't help but smile at her choice of moniker for him.

"When you get to be my age, honey, it's a little trickier to keep it spicy, so I have to get creative." She winks at me, taking a sip from her cup.

"He gets worried about me a lot these days. Oh, I can't fault him for it, though. Not after what happened to Lucille." She leans back against the cushion of the booth, daintily holding her cup in one hand while she blots the corner of her mouth with a napkin. Careful not to smear her bright red lipstick.

"My poor friend Lucille. When you're older, honey, there aren't many people to take care of you. To worry about your whereabouts. We have to take care of each other. I call Lucille every day at five o'clock sharp. She knows to answer the phone, so I know she's home safe for the evening. Well, one day, there was no answer. I called up my lover and had him drive me past her home— he sees better at night than I do— but her car was missing."

"Oh, my, that's awful! Did you find her? Is she alright?" I exclaim.

She nods. "Yes. It took several days and calls to the police station and hospitals. You know they won't tell you anything if you aren't a blood relative. I finally lied and said I was her sister. Come to find out, she had fallen in the parking lot of the grocery store and hit her head. The poor thing was holed up in a nursing home! We were so relieved when we found her. I was beginning to think she might have been dead."

My coffee cup freezes midair as I take in her statement. *Almost presumed dead*, but she was actually in the nursing home. A perfect place to stash a person and then go on pretending they are dead...

Chapter 16

Hope

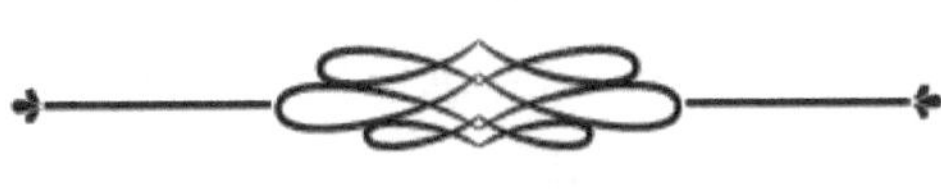

TIME IS FICKLE, ETERNITY versus a second. All in the eye of the beholder. Time held me captive, caused me grief, and loomed over me with strangling dominion. I longed to cease. Now, eternity has become my blessing. Every second is its own thriving pulse of joy, pumping a renewed sense of purpose into me. I am free. I am complete. She completes me, soldering the cracks, so that despair can no longer leak my soul.

I bask in the feel of Willow in my arms, her softness, her life. Perhaps it's foolish, thinking we could grow old together— or at least she could be happy with me by her side as she experiences life. I could use the garage as a small shop? I could make custom wood furniture to help support us, and then she wouldn't have to work so hard at the coffee shop. I might be a little rusty, but I don't think it would take much to hone my skills again.

Sure, I would continue to help out at Dripping too. I could manage the kitchen area where no one would see items floating around. She'd never have to lift a finger around the house. I can take care of her. Unorthodox, yes, but we could make it work.

She stirs and checks her phone. I can't see who's calling, but she becomes a whirlwind around the bedroom. Frantically snatching up her clothing and her keys, she's out the door before I can get her attention, leaving me behind.

It's still early morning, the sun has risen, but the sky is still cast in a low hue, brisk fall air crisping through the trees. I check the front porch, but she's already gone. Something isn't right. She wouldn't have forgotten Humphrey like that. We've gone everywhere together since her last visit to Madame Ophelia.

Anger and shame fill my chest. Who am I kidding, thinking I can take care of her? What use am I to her? What did I think I would add to her life? Doubt takes hold like a lead weight where hope had just floated. I wander into the backyard, to the oak tree I've grown fond of. The curse of being tied to Humphrey; I'll never fully be the man she needs. A protector or a provider...

I hear the hard slam of a door from the front porch. Has she already returned? This isn't right. I feel... strange; something pulls at me, ripping me from the yard into blackness. "No, no— No, no, no, no. This isn't right! This isn't how I was supposed to leave! I'm not ready, I'm not ready!"

Pleading with the universe as devastation constricts my heart like a vice— I can't leave her like this, she won't understand— "Willow!" I wail into the darkness, tears filling my eyes. I scrub my hands down my face as I lie in anguish in the dark. "I take it all back... All the years I begged for this... I take it all back..."

CHAPTER 17
RECOMPENSE

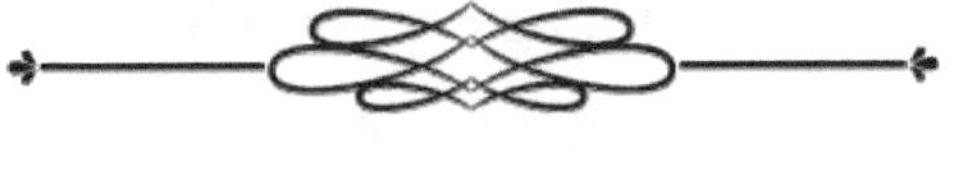

Gerald

THUNDER CRASHES BETWEEN DARK clouds, shaking the windows. It's followed by lightning that illuminates my shitty apartment like a spotlight coming through. The sudden bright flashes clashing against the otherwise pitch-black space. The power went out on this block about an hour ago. I got one flashlight with dead batteries.

Probably best to sit in the dark anyway; makes it harder for someone looking up from the street to see if I'm up here. I press my back against the wall next to the window. There're no curtains or blinds to pull closed. I feel like a sitting duck up here. Three apartments and a new burner phone every two weeks made no difference. He still finds me.

The buzz of an incoming text has become the most horrific sound these days. My spine stiffens at the sound. The messages have been incessant and blood chilling, heralding my impending doom.

Uknown: UR up to 784K

Unknown: shoulda paid on time G

After the lowball offer I got for that house— dumbass real estate agent, I knew he was a loser— and the cash from the estate sale, I'm still $1K short of the *original* debt. I took that fucking bottle Mother coddled all those years to the antiques dealer— worthless. FUCK! I almost smashed it right there in his office. It wouldn't have mattered anyway, even if it was worth billions, if I didn't get the cash in hand. He wants every penny in full. Maybe I can convince him that it's valuable? He could take it as collateral. Buy me a little more time...

You're a loser, Gerald. You can't hold a job. You can't win a bet. Why should I expect you're good for it anymore? I want everything I'm owed. You got me.

His words from that phone call echo in my head. It's like he's standing right here, looming over my shoulder all the time.

If you don't pay, well, it won't be quick, and it won't be pretty.

I scrub my hands down my face and dig my nails into the hollows of my cheeks, the bite of pain taking some edge off the fear. I need a drink; fuck might as well drink myself to death. It would probably be a better experience than what he's got coming for me.

I pull a bottle of cheap whiskey and a glass from the cabinet. Unsteady, I fumble the glass, and it smashes on the kitchen floor. My hands, fuck, if they could just stop shaking. I give up on pouring and just slug straight from the bottle, the burn sliding into my stomach, slowly dulling the doom that's making my heart race.

This wasn't supposed to be my life. I was gonna do something big, go back to law school, or work my way up the corporate ladder. Slumming it to hide from loan sharks is beneath me. What would

Mother think of me? The slam of a door from down the hallway makes me jump, and I damn near drop the bottle; whiskey sloshes all over the floor. I scrub my hand down my face. He can't be here yet, can he? How could he have gotten in?

Slow as I can manage, I slide the whiskey bottle back onto the countertop and pull the big butcher knife from the drawer. The floor of this shitty apartment creaks with each step I take toward the hall. With no electricity, there isn't a chance in hell of seeing anything down there. Stopping at the entrance, I wait and listen, but the thunder and the rain pelting the apartment windows are too loud to hear any subtle sounds of movement.

There are only two doorways, the bathroom and the bedroom. The bathroom door is still open, so that leaves...

Sliding my feet along the carpet, I try to minimize the creak of my movements. I still can't hear any sounds over the rain, but this is where he's gotta be. I lift my boot and kick in the bedroom door, knife raised and howling like a madman as I burst into the room. Nothing. There's nobody in here. The closet... Again, I kick the door in and then jump back in case he's got a gun, but it's dark and empty. I angrily kick around the few boxes I have stashed in here. "JUST FUCKING SHOW YOURSELF DAMNIT!!" I don't want this cat-and-mouse game. Enraged, I rip the sheets from the bed and toss the mattress; nobody under there. "FUCK YOU!"

Next, it's the bathroom. I sweep the counter of my toothbrush and comb, rip the shower curtain down, and snap the rod over my knee. "MOTHER FUCKER! IF YOU WANT ME, HERE I AM!"

Despair, excruciating despair, slithers over my body. "I'm sorry, Mother, I never meant to fuck up like this…" I was gonna get it all back, the money, my reputation, the house. Fuck you, Ricky, you greedy bastard! Every time I saved up a little, he'd be there. Whispering like a devil on my shoulder about the next big payday. He always had a guy or a scheme that was gonna get us loads of money. And look at how it all turned out. He schemed himself right into a grave, dragging me behind him.

I stumble back down the hallway to the kitchen, snag my bottle by the neck, and slug again, downing a third of it in one swallow, then spew it all back out as the silhouette of a man forms in the doorway. "Where the fuck did you come from?" I whisper. The kitchen cabinet doors begin to slam open and closed chaotically. The sudden noise makes me jump, and I lose my grip on the bottle.

It smashes on the linoleum at my feet; I chance taking my eyes off the shadowy figure to a glance downward. The shards levitate and swirl, encircling me. "Who, who the fuck are you?!" I test the whirlpool of glass with my hand and jerk it back as my skin gets sliced open. The blood, warm and sticky, seeps into my white t-shirt as I clutch my mangled hand to my chest. Fractured pieces of glass begin shooting out of the whirlpool and slashing at me, erratically slicing at the skin of my face and arms.

Dribbles of blood cascade down my body. "Leave me the fuck alone you psycho!" I drop to my knees and attempt to crawl out from underneath the spiral, slipping on the bloody linoleum and the glass shards still on the floor. Sharp edges continue to slice at my ears and my back as I try to escape.

Snot and tears mix with the blood rolling down my chin. I slip and fall on my stomach, using my elbows to pull myself. A pathetic sob escapes me as I watch in horror; the mangled hands and face of my clock float before me, the hands spinning round and round. I desperately try to reach the bathroom. Kicking the door closed with my feet, I lay on my back, panting. What the FUCK was that? This can't be real!

Inside the bathroom is a stark contrast to the storm I left outside. Silence, too much silence. Like sound was sucked out of the air. The sounds of the storm are gone, not even my heavy breathing or pounding heart registers in my ears. Then it's broken by the gritty sound of metal turning. I turn my eyes toward it to see the hot water knob on the shower twisting.

Scalding water begins to spray from the shower head. Filling the room with thick steam. Then comes the squeaking from above the sink. I watch in horror as invisible fingers write on the foggy mirror... *you're done.*

CHAPTER 18

MELEE

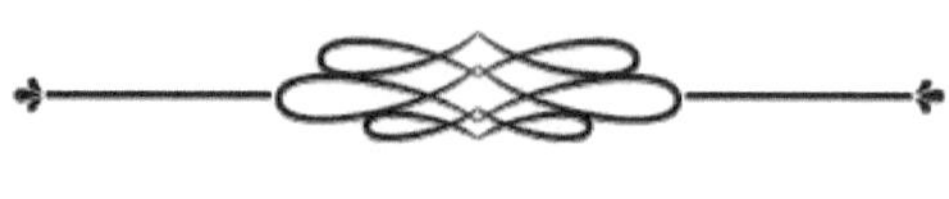

Willow

I PULL MY SUV back up to my house, excited to tell Freddy about my conversation with Dorthia. What I found tore my heart out. My screaming brought Mrs. Graham over with her pistol in hand. I collapsed into her arms, sobbing incoherently into her fuzzy pink bathrobe. She called the police for me and gave a description of the creeper she had seen in the neighborhood. When they asked me the estimated value of what was taken, I told them it was priceless.

My front entrance table was smashed to bits, all my little figures shattered and stomped on. It was clear what they were after. Humphrey had been chilling on my kitchen island that morning. He was gone, and the destruction of my house went no further. After the police left, Mrs. Graham offered to help clean up. She also offered to help hide a body if I ever needed that, too. God love her. If I knew who, and it could bring Freddy back, I'd take her up on that offer.

I lay on the floor of my living room, staring at the ceiling and trying to slow my gasping breaths. Tears stream from the corners of my eyes, and I can't stop crying. I can't go down like this. I can't lose him. We were so close, we were going to set him free. My heart cracks, and I hyperventilate, choking, silent sobs wracking my body. I'm not sure how long I have been lying on the carpet, listless. My mother's ringtone blares into the silence. She just keeps calling, not getting the hint. I don't even have the energy to get up. I work the phone from my back pocket, press speaker, and toss it onto the floor next to me.

"Willow," she barks. "Willow, I can hear your breathing. You sound like a tired dog; stop that."

"Mom, it's not really a good time," I answer.

"It's never a good time to speak to your mother." She huffs. "I'm calling because I found you someone and set you up a date. He's a very nice young man—"

I cut her off right there. Anger erupted in my voice. "Mom, I don't need one of your show ponies!" I cover my face with my hands as a fresh wave of tears floods my eyes. I only need Freddy.

"Willow, I don't want to hear this 'I don't need a man' blabbering again. I will not let my daughter wallow in misery and loneliness. I did not raise you to wallow..."

I don't hear whatever she says after that. For once, my mother has some wise words. She's right, I am not a wallower, I am a DOER!

Leaving her voice trailing on, I jolt up from the floor. Wiping my wet cheeks and rifling for my keys, determination taking over the defeat in my chest. I am wasting precious time when I could be looking for him! It can't end like this. We can't end like this. I won't allow it. I hang up on my mother and rush back out to my car. The plan is foggy in my mind, but getting clearer with each step.

There are twenty-five nursing homes in the city. I play the same grift at each one. Walking up to the nurses' station and using the most innocent expression and voice I can muster in my present condition. "Hi, I'm here to visit my grandmother, Edith Grant."

Now, I'm standing in front of the one with the lowest rating. I should have figured that, if you stash someone away, you probably are paying top dollar for their care. I started at the swankiest on the list and worked my way down. Assuming that Edith would be at a nice facility based on her estate sale, but if you wanted to forget someone was alive... this is the place.

I try not to look disgusted by the smell as I approach the nurses' desk. "Hello, I'm here to visit my grandmother, Edith Grant?" Without even looking up at me, the attendant points down the hallway, "Activities room."

"Thank you," I say and hurry down the hallway with my heart in my throat. I found her! I have pictures of her from her youth that I saved from the internet. I hope I can recognize her. I was thinking she would be in a room by herself, but if I have to pick her out of a group, it may give me away.

My red sneakers squeak on the sticky linoleum. An elderly lady in a wheelchair uses the handrail to pull herself up the hallway, calling out for her nurse. Everything about this place feels sad and forgotten. I wonder how many of the residents are without family to visit them or make sure they are being cared for properly.

As I turn the corner into the Activities Room, I slow my pace. I slip down the length of the wall near the entrance and take a moment to scan the room for potential Ediths.

"Who are you here to see, dear?"

I nearly jump out of my skin as the nurse materializes to my right. "Oh, uh, I'm looking for my grandmother, Edith Grant? I'm sorry, I haven't seen her in years because I live out of state." The lie rolls off my tongue, convincingly, I hope.

"Oh, she'll be so thrilled to have you visit, sweetheart, and you're in luck, she's having a real clear day. Right over there, at the table with the puzzles." The nurse pats my shoulder before passing me to go check on another resident.

There at a table, toward the right side of the room, is a small woman with smooth grey hair pulled into a short ponytail. Her back is to me, a pretty floral shawl draped over her shoulders. I take a wide berth to approach so I don't startle her and to give myself a little more time to conjure some bravery.

What if she won't talk to me? What if she tells them I'm not her granddaughter? What if she calls security? What if I never find Freddy? That last question has my feet moving. I pull out the chair next to her, force a smile to cover the fear on my face, and sit down. "Hey, that's a pretty puzzle. Do you mind if I watch you put it together?"

Her head pops up in surprise. She hesitates for only a second before a big smile grows on her lips. "Oh, hello, do you like puzzles?" Her hand reaches out to pat mine and gives me a kind little squeeze.

"Not particularly, I've never been very good at them, no patience." I laugh.

"I hate these bastard puzzles, but there's not bloody else to do in this place." She grins happily, her expression a mismatch for her assessment of her leisure activity.

"My name is Edith, it's nice to meet you. Whoever you are." She turns back to her work, handing me an end piece to place.

"I'm Willow, it's so nice to finally meet you, Edith." This feels surreal. A few months ago, I was searching for her obituary before I went to her estate sale. Now, I'm sitting here with her, doing an ugly puzzle of kittens in a basket of laundry. We work silently for a long while. I'm not sure how to start this conversation. *Hey, do you remember a young, handsome man who got spiritually kidnapped into a bottle at your shop? Well, I fell in love with him, and then I lost him. Can you help me find him?*

Yeah, I don't think that will work. I don't know what information I thought I would gain here. Before I knew Freddy was gone, I imagined bringing Humphrey along if I ever found her. But now? Even if she remembered the bottle, how was she going to help me find who took him?

"That's a heavy sigh, dear. What's on your mind?" She looks up from her work, her blue eyes, faded with age, big and sincere. "OH, um, I'm having man problems.... I thought I had found my soul mate, but I lost him..." I stare at the exit sign on the far wall while I fight my tears.

"Are you sure he's lost?" She asks.

"Well, more like someone stole him," I say.

"Oh, that's terrible. You seem like a nice young woman. I can feel it. I'm very intuitive, you know. You'll find your happily ever after. I can feel it." She squeezes my hand again and passes me a wadded-up tissue.

"Are you having a nice visit with your granddaughter, Edith?" The nurse has come by to check on us. She pats Edith on the shoulder and smiles down at us. Panic pumps through my veins. This is it, I'm about to be dragged out of this place like a criminal. Can you go to jail for sneaking into a nursing home to visit elderly people?

"Oh, no, this isn't my granddaughter. I don't have any grandchildren. This is my new friend, Willow." Edith looks back and forth between the nurse and me. I hold my breath, bracing for the fallout. The nurse just looks over Edith's shoulder at me with a sympathetic expression. Then says, "How about I get you two some coffee," and walks away.

Whew, that was close. I watch the nurse as she goes to a rolling cart at the back of the room and fills up some paper cups with what is probably super watered-down coffee. Edith starts talking again. "I only have one son, I'd set you a date, but I don't think he's the kind of man you'd like, dear. Always in trouble, that one." She reaches into her shawl to retrieve a small photo book.

The little book is labeled on the front, Edith's Memory Album. She flips it open to show me pictures of her family. The photos have all been tagged with a label maker with the person's name, relationship to Edith, and the year of their birth and death.

Edith proudly shows off her late husband; his picture is from his youth before they moved from London. It makes me think of Freddy's young face from the newspaper article. The last picture in the album is a little boy; the birth date indicates that he would be an adult now, older than me.

"This is my Gerald. He was a sweet little boy. But he's gotten himself in trouble over the years..." She turns the photo sleeve over, revealing a picture of grown-up Gerald. "It doesn't matter what your children get themselves into; you still love them and wish them the best."

Something seems oddly familiar about this picture. It isn't a current image, but it is of Gerald as an adult. He looks young and optimistic here. Edith is still telling me all about her son.

"Wasn't he handsome? Looks so much like his father here. This is before he got that bad scar on his cheek," she brushes her finger over his left cheek in the photo. "That was the first time I knew he was headed down a terrible path. He had been dismissed from his university and got himself into some gambling troubles. I tried to help him as much as I could. He got into an awful brawl downtown... arrested, too. That cut on his cheek didn't heal well."

The nurse places the coffee and a few cookies on the table for us while we visit. I stay with Edith for two more hours, learning about her life, living in London, her curiosity shop... She talks until she gets tired. I walk her back to her room and help her get settled into her bed for a nap.

After promising that I would come back and visit another day, I pull the door slightly to cut down the noise from the hallway so she can rest. As I turn to leave, I pass the nurse from the activities room. She reaches out her hand to my shoulder, "Don't let it hurt your feelings that she didn't recognize you, honey, that's just the way it is when they have Dementia. I know it can be hard to stomach when your family member doesn't know you anymore."

Tears prick my eyes. Poor Edith, having to live with the confusion and anxiety that comes with this disease. The nurse leans in to hug me, still thinking I'm a grieving granddaughter. I can be Edith's granddaughter. I won't let her be forgotten in this run-down facility.

As I drive away, my stomach churns. Maybe it's the torrential emotions from losing Freddy and seeing the conditions Edith is enduring, but I have this nagging sense that I've missed something. That photograph of Gerald lingers in my mind's eye. I'm not closer to finding Freddy, and now I'm not sure what to do next. It will be weeks, or longer, probably before the police find who broke into my house, if they find them.

I drive over to Dripping. I need a place to sit and think. I click the locks in place behind me as I set my bag down in my office and head to the kitchen. I think better when my hands are busy, so I start pulling out fruit to slice up for tomorrow's service.

How do I open this place and go to work like it's any other Tuesday when I don't have Freddy? My mind drifts to how much my life has changed since I bought that bottle. Memories bleeding into and out of focus. Being scared, thinking my coffee shop was going to burn down, realizing I was being haunted... falling for a ghost.

My gut churns again as realization hits. That picture of Gerald, young, carefree Gerald. Gerald, before all his troubles made him look road-hardened and worn. Gerald with a scar on his left cheek— my mystery customer! The gruff guy; he left his coffee behind... and he likes antiques! Shit! I drop the knife and leave the fruit and everything right there on the counter.

The engine of my SUV roars as I floor my accelerator, my grip on the steering wheel blanching my fingers. I can't get back home fast enough. Now that the realization has hit, I can't unsee it. I'm whipping through traffic and flying down the freeway to my exit. It's got to be him.

Thank God, Mrs. Graham is a stay-at-home chain smoker. She's sitting on her porch, bathrobe and curlers, smoking her one hundredth cigarette for the day. She's calmly perched on the porch ledge like she's been waiting for me to come over for coffee. I'm racing up her steps, already out of breath like I ran all the way home instead of speeding like a demon.

I'm doubled over and wheezing from my panic as I scroll through my phone. Edith may not have had a digital footprint to search, but Gerald sure as hell did. Stretching my arm out, I turn the phone toward Mrs. Graham.

"Imagine— huh— this guy— huh— older and fugglier— huh— and with a scar..." I can barely get the description out as I brandish a picture of Gerald I found on the internet.

With her cigarette left hanging between her dry, hot-pink lips, she holds my phone with both hands and stretches it back, squinting one eye and trying to determine who this is.

"Yep, honey, that's the rat bastard for sure."

I snatch the phone back from Mrs. Graham and immediately dial Krista. She picks up on the third ring.

"Hey, it's been a few days, bitch. What's been going on?" she answers.

Mrs. Graham calmly smokes her cigarette, still seated on the ledge of her porch, like I'm not acting like a complete psycho right now.

"Krista, I need a favor."

"Do I get my car or my shovel?" she responds.

"Maybe both; this is a secret. You can't involve Jolie, yet." Jolie is a peaceful voice of reason; she'd never go along with this. "Okay...," Krista waits for my explanation.

"You and Lawrence are tight, huh? I need an address. Gerald Grant. I'll explain later."

"You got it, I'll call you back when I have it."

I end the call and start pacing Mrs. Graham's porch, a plan taking form in my mind. I can't go to the police, it will take them too long to act. He could sell the bottle off to someone, and I'd never get Freddy back. I can't ask Jolie and her fiancé for help yet, either. He would lose his shit and try to stop me.

Mrs. Graham spits on the end of her cigarette, then stubs it out in her ashtray. "You go get your man, baby. Tell me all about it after you're done." She heads back into her house, the bang of her screen door nailing my resolve into place.

Six days. That's how long it's been since I lost Freddy. It's just after sunset. The night settles over Lawrence's dark, nondescript sedan like a camouflage blanket. There are no streetlights here.

No pedestrians out for a stroll in this neighborhood after dark either, for good reasons. I was going to come alone, but Krista and Lawrence refused. He held the address hostage until I agreed to let them accompany me. They made a good point. If this went upside down and they knew what I'd done... let's just say Lawrence would probably end up in a lake somewhere, and Jolie would never forgive Krista.

So here we are, staking out the crappy second-floor apartment that is registered to an Edward Grant. The problem is that Edward Grant has been dead for a long ass time, but his son, Gerald, is in hiding. Lawrence also uncovered that Gerald has a substantial debt to a local loan shark. Explains a lot about his behavior.

During my visit with Edith at the nursing home, she told me all about the curiosity shop she had back in London. Her favorite item in the entire shop: a little wine decanter. She described Humphrey perfectly. Going on and on about how sentimental that little man was, her most prized possession. I can only assume that Gerald mistook her affection for the piece as actual monetary value, as to why he would try to steal it back.

"Okay, I'll go up and ask for it back. You two stay here." Lawrence says as he reaches for the door handle.

"Abso-fucking-lutely not. This is personal. I will get Humphrey back." I use my best girlboss bitch voice that I learned from Krista. I need to know Freddy is around. What if something happened after he was stolen, and Lawrence brings back an empty Humphrey?

"And I will go with both of you," Krista adds from the front passenger seat. We've had this argument for the last few hours; he won't win, and he knows it.

"You girls are gonna get me skinned alive, you know that?" Lawrence resigns.

The three of us exit the car, shutting the doors as quietly as possible so as not to give ourselves away.

"If this asshat is hiding from loan sharks, then he's gonna be on edge. You follow my lead and don't do anything rash or stupid, understood?" He's looking dead at me when he barks his order. That's fair. I'm definitely in tiger mode, ready to strike the moment I lay eyes on this guy. I'm armed with pepper spray, a Kubaton, and my rape whistle. I've been mentally refreshing the techniques I learned that summer I took up kickboxing at the Y. I'm channeling my inner badass, and I'm prepared to do whatever it takes to get Freddy back.

The dim fluorescent light flickers overhead, bathing the stairwell in foreboding. The handrail is peeling and rusty, rust and water stains paint the walls and steps. We slip single file behind Lawrence up to the second floor. When we reach the landing, Lawrence goes first, peeking around the doorframe to make sure it's clear before waving us on. When we finally reach the apartment, he puts his finger over his lips to shush us, even though we were already silent. I glance over at Krista, in her cut-off jean shorts, fishnet tights, and combat boots, she looks like a total femme fatale, her face confident, eyes focused.

I try to draw from her energy to calm my raw nerves. I can't stop worrying about Freddy. He must be scared and confused. He's probably wondering why I just took off that day without him, and then some grubby stranger stole him away. I can't wait until I'm holding Humphrey safely in my arms and bringing Freddy back to my house.

Lawrence moves to the opposite side of the door, out of sight from the peephole, and knocks softly. It's silent in the apartment. He may not even be home.

I make "urgent eyes" at Lawrence, who returns my expression with an eye roll. He reaches across the door and tries the knob; miraculously, it turns. He presses his palm to the door and pushes it open a few inches. Through the cracked opening, I see him, Humphrey, the corner of the little statue just visible through the entryway to the living area. What else I see is like a horror movie.

Fighting the urge to rush through the door to him, I let Lawrence enter first. The three of us, again in single file, slip around the doorframe and into the entryway of the apartment. We hug the wall to avoid the destruction of shattered glass and blood splatter. Furniture is splintered around the carpet, and the apartment reeks of alcohol and urine. Soft sobbing drifts from down the hallway. I pass a worried look toward my friends.

Lawrence whispers, "Let's just grab the statue and get out. We can call 911 after we get back to the car." Krista and I nod in agreement, following closely behind him as we inch toward the living area.

He's right there. I'm so close to having him back. My heart is in my throat, and my breath has gone shallow. Lawrence slips closer to the living room. This part of the apartment appears to be empty, the only sign of life being the sobbing coming from the back.

Lawrence slinks forward and wraps his fingers around the head of the statue. He passes it backward to me, keeping his eyes forward, looking out for danger. I hug Humphrey to my heart, so grateful to have him back in my hands. Krista and I turn around to head back through the apartment door, only to see a group of men blocking our exits. Holy shit balls, what do we do now? I squeeze Humphrey protectively to my chest. Lawrence puts a hand on Krista's and my shoulder. We back ourselves into the living room as the men enter the apartment, guns drawn.

"Gerald!" The mystery man calls out into the apartment. "Time's up! Get out here, or your little friends are gonna join you in your fate."

Lawrence moves around us to stand protectively in front of Krista and me. The sobbing from down the hallway gets louder. Shuffling and grunting, a man, Gerald, comes lumbering down the hallway toward us. He looks like shit, blood dripping down his face, chest, and legs. I don't know what's happened in this apartment, but it was terrifying, and I'm afraid it's about to get worse.

As Gerald gets closer, I see the shock on his face at seeing me in his apartment. Will he throw us to the wolves? He limps forward, hugging his arms to his stomach. It's hard to tell where his wounds are because there is so much blood. I have to look away. I huddle closer to Krista and Lawrence. I hope I haven't walked my friends to a death sentence.

"I got you something, Mr. McBride. I got something worth a lot, just take it somewhere and you can see how much it's worth." He leans against the edge of the hallway entrance, huffing, snot and saliva running down his lips and chin.

"I don't give a FUCK what you got, Gerald. You missed the deadline, and now you're a *deadman*." Mr. McBride waves his gun at one of his henchmen, who moves toward Gerald, grabbing him by the arm and pulling him further into the living room.

Lawrence clears his throat, "McBride, you know who I am?" He studies Lawrence, then me, then Krista, and back to Lawrence. "Yeah, I know ya. Wouldn't expect you to be mixed up with this lowlife."

"If you know me, then you know who I work for. We just want to walk out of here, no trouble, and no opinion on your business with this man." Lawrence's voice is measured. Conveying respect but assertiveness. I hold my breath, waiting for the verdict. Can my friends and I walk out of here unscathed? I'm so focused on Mr. McBride as he rubs his chin in contemplation that I don't notice Gerald at first.

He lunges at me from the side, trying to snatch Humphrey from my hands. I grip the statue with all my might, refusing to let him go again. Lawrence and Krista hang on to my arms, trying to keep me close to them. Krista's arms wrap around my waist to help hold me up. I kick and claw at Gerald, tugging back on Humphrey. I'll be fucking damned before I let him go.

Gerald is screaming hysterically. "The statue, it's worth millions, it has magic powers! Take it, McBride, just take it! I swear it will cover my debt!!"

I wrap my arms around Humphrey as tightly as I can. Gerald and I are locked in a tug-of-war. Lawrence and Krista pull on my body, trying to break me apart from this madman. Gerald falls to his knees, tugging with all his might on Humphrey. With one final hard tug, he rips Humphrey from my arms. Throwing himself toward Mr. McBride's feet, offering him the bottle like a sacrifice. I break free from Lawrence and Krista and throw my body on top of his, scratching and clawing his hands to pry Humphrey free. We roll around the dirty carpet, grappling for control.

I can feel other hands pulling at my body and indiscriminate yelling from other voices in the room. I can't give up, I can't lose him. I stick my fingers into Gerald's eye socket, trying anything I can to get him to let go. A gunshot stuns everything into silence. McBride snatches the statue from Gerald's hands and lifts him overhead.

"I don't give a FUCK! You'll pay with your fucking life! This isn't about money anymore, Gerald, it's a message about crossing me." He smashes Humphrey to the ground, the statue splintering into shards, mixing with the broken furniture and blood already soiling the carpet.

"NNNNNOOOOOOOOOOOO!" I scream and sink to the floor in agony. Running my hands through the shards, I try desperately to put him back together. "FREDDY!" I scream his name again and again. Scooping up as many pieces of Humphrey as I can, raking them toward me.

As I try fruitlessly to put his face back together, I feel it. The hand on my cheek. Warm and comforting, it lingers a moment, just long enough for me to raise my hand to join his, then fades away.

I wail in anguish, oblivious to the chaos that ensues around me. I can't lose him, I can't, I can't ...

I don't feel Lawrence lift me in his arms, I don't feel myself being hauled downstairs or being placed in the backseat of the sedan. All I feel is heartbreak. And I can't imagine a future where I feel anything else. The lights of the city blur past us. The fragments of Humphrey's face lay in my lap. I lean my head against the window of the backseat, tears streaming down my face. My friends' voices blur around me. I vaguely register Krista calling my name, but it doesn't matter what she has to say. Nothing matters anymore, not without Freddy.

CHAPTER 19
DEJECTION

I FAILED. I FAILED him. The thought consumes me. Like an anvil around my neck, the weight of this guilt is unbearable. Krista walks me into the front door of my house, my arm slung over her shoulder for support. She wanted to take me to her house, but I refused. I need to be where I was last with Freddy.

The night before the robbery, the love making, the bliss, him holding me through the night, waking up in his arms, all of that. The teasing hints of woodsy smells and soft, phantom touches. I need to be near it. I need to reach into the past and pull him back to me.

Spent candles that I never cleaned up still line the tops of my dresser and nightstand. The image of my reflection suspended in the air in ecstasy haunts my mirror. Every day, I have paced my room, reliving our last night together with urgency and desperation for his return. Whispering promises to the universe that I would protect and cherish him for the rest of my life if it would return him to me.

My fingers grapple and search for the edge of my blankets, trying to cocoon myself in them as if to replicate his embrace, the way I have every night he's been missing and the way I will every night for the rest of my life. I try sniffing the pillow where he would have lain next to me, but of course, I can only smell myself. I press it into my face and wail into the fabric. If I suffocate and die, can I be with him? I wrap my arms around it and try to push it as far as I can into my face. I don't want to breathe anymore. I don't want to think or feel anymore. I only want Freddy. My Freddy.

"Jesus, Willow!" Krista grabs the edge of the pillow and begins to jerk it out from under my hands. I pull down on it with all my might. She finally breaks it free, and my face jerks back, then falls into the mattress.

"Willow, what the hell? I know you were attached to him, but I thought you wanted him to be free? To pass on?" She rubs my back sympathetically. She's trying to be comforting; she really is, but right now, I loathe the idea of being comforted.

"I wanted him to be happy, to find peace…" I sob into my mattress. "But I'm a selfish bitch and I wanted him to find all that with me!"

"What?" She lowers herself down on my bed, lying next to me, looking up at the ceiling while I continue trying to suffocate my broken heart.

"Okay, I know this may sound outrageous. I fell in love with my ghost. And I wanted— I thought maybe— I don't know what I thought. Madame Ophelia said he wasn't an ordinary ghost." I flip over on my side to face Krista, letting the tears flow freely down my nose and cheeks.

"I am not fit for a normal relationship. I have never belonged in regular civilized society. I'm the freaky girl who likes dark shit. Or, I'm a poser cause I'm not freaky enough. Even the other freaky people don't really want me in their ranks." I take a strangled breath in and try to calm my voice so I can get my words out.

"It's not like I haven't tried to fit in, be normal. But I went on this date my mom set up—"

"Fuck off, you did not! We talked about this, Willow. You were committed to maintaining strong boundaries with your mom." Krista punches my arm as she scolds me.

"Not the point, right now. And that hurt." I whine.

"Okay, I'm sorry. Please continue." She rolls to her side to fully face me.

"I went on this date, the night before the farmers market thing. And it was awful, and he just wanted to get laid and told me I would never be wife material for a guy like him, just a fun time. And that's what they all say. And I was getting more comfortable with Freddy, and he is so caring, and thoughtful, and... I just felt like we made sense, you know." I start to cry again. Krista lies silently next to me, giving me space to fall to pieces.

"I know I sound crazy, but my feelings for him are real and they are deep and I need him, Krista, I need him." She wraps her arms around me as I cry, rubbing my back and shushing me gently.

"Okay," she sighs deeply. "I'm going to tell you the same thing I told Jolie when she confessed to being in love with her stalker. I will never judge you. I want you to find happiness and have your needs met. The important thing is that you are happy, and *you* feel loved, and *you* know your worth." I start another round of racking sobs.

"Willow, you are not a square peg in the round hole of normal society. You are a— a supernova that the world tries to put in a bottle. You are so amazing, it is unreal... *supernatural*, and if a supernatural boyfriend is what your heart desires, then… I don't really know how to finish that sentence. I love you, but this sounds even weirder out loud."

I have to laugh at her honesty, and it feels good to have a small moment of reprieve from heartbreak. We giggle together at my own weirdo expense, but only for a moment because the cold, hard truth is— "I lost him, Krista." My voice cracks; I can barely get the words out. "He's never coming back."

I roll back toward the safety of my friend's embrace. How does my life move forward without Fredrick?

Fuck, my fingers are stuck together again. I take my other hand and force them apart. Yesterday, Lawrence showed up with a paper bag holding the rest of Humphrey. I cried on his shoulder for a good twenty minutes. I didn't even ask how he got the pieces back. Or what happened to Gerald, for that matter.

I'm stationed at my kitchen countertop, struggling to glue him back together. I have to keep telling myself that it won't bring Freddy back, but I need to show care for Humphrey, a way to memorialize the colossal loss I feel.

I shut Dripping down for the week; it's gonna suck, but I have money in savings, and I can't even fathom trying to function at work right now. I can't fathom changing my pajamas right now. Krista and Jolie have been taking shifts coming to sit with me. It is annoying as fuck; I want to grieve in private. I am grateful for their support, though. They don't try to force me to be happy, but they do force me to eat and brush my hair.

Jolie completely lost her shit on Krista and me after she found out what we did. I didn't know she could get mad like that. I think Lawrence got it bad from her fiancé, too. He's kind of adopted us as little sisters. I should have asked him to help me. Maybe if I hadn't been so determined to get Freddy back myself, he would have made it home in one piece. God, this is all my fault. Why did I leave him behind that day? I was so stupid.

I'm happy for Jolie. She deserved to find her person. I haven't been jealous of her happiness one bit until now. Now, I want to vomit every time I think of them living happily ever after, riding off into the sunset hand in hand. A forever love that I'll never enjoy because mine literally smashed to the floor.

I place another piece of Humphrey's body together. He has shoulders now. It's taking me forever to glue him because I can't see straight from all the crying. His little shards are all crookedly placed. Maybe I can get some ceramic paint and touch him up so the cracks aren't so obvious.

Knocking on my front door startles me, and I nearly knock Humphrey over and smash him all over again. Part of me wants to pretend I'm not home, but I know that it won't fly when my friends have professional hackers on speed dial.

The knocking persists. I wonder which one of my friends has come to babysit today. It's probably Jolie because Krista would have barged in by now. I trudge over to the door and begrudgingly open it. "Mrs. Graham?" I'm surprised to see her. I think I've only ever talked to her when she's on her front porch smoking. Well... except the day Humphrey was stolen.

Also, there's no cigarette hanging from her lips. The curlers and robe are still in place. I don't know if she owns other clothes. "Hey, baby, I brought ya some glue." She pushes past me like she's been in my house enough to be family. Stunned, it takes me a moment to shut the door and follow her to the kitchen, where she's admiring my handy work on Humphrey.

"Mrs. Graham, that's really nice of you, but how did you know I needed glue?" I ask.

"Just had an inkling, baby." She picks up a piece of Humphrey's face and admires him. I have to squeeze my fingernails into my palms. I don't really want anyone to touch him but me. Even if it is Mrs. Graham.

"Relax, sugar, I'm not gonna hurt him." She places the piece back on the counter and turns to help herself to the coffee maker. Opening the cabinet and getting cups and coffee pods, I stare at her from behind.

I've never spoken to her in depth, always passing pleasantries while I came and went on my own missions. She's been a permanent fixture on her front porch. Always dressed like she's getting ready for something, but never actually ready. For three years, I've considered her a neighborly friend, but I've never actually taken the time to get to know her.

She fixes her coffee and then turns back to me, taking a seat on the barstool next to mine. She takes a little sip from her mug, staring off toward the far wall. We sit in silence together. Her sipping coffee, and me gluing Humphrey back together like a bad nursery rhyme.

"This might be the first time I haven't had a cigarette in my mouth since 1976." She breaks the silence.

"That's a long time, Mrs. Graham. Are you thinking about quitting?" I pause my gluing to give her my attention.

"Probably should. I picked up my first cigarette on the evening of September 17th. It was a Friday night, and I was waiting for my husband to come home from work. We had planned a night out. He never came home. I picked up his pack of smokes and lit one up. I've been waiting out on that porch ever since... He swerved to miss a deer and landed his car in the ditch. I think I felt it in my soul, you know, when he left this earth."

She stares down into the mug as if the memory is playing on the creamed liquid screen. "I would give anything to be with him again; he was my one true love. So, I figure I've got an idea of what you're feeling right now." She pats my leg gently. "He was a good one."

She's made little statements like that before, things that made sense but also didn't. "Mrs. Graham, could you see Freddy?"

She turns her shoulders toward me. Coffee cup raised in one hand and her other wrapped around her waist, her face indignant. "Of course, I could see him. I'm your nosy neighbor, it's my job to know all your business."

"Yeah, but how did you see him?"

"Baby, I've been waiting for a ghost to show up at my front door for forty-nine years. You think I wouldn't notice if one moved into the next house?" She finishes her coffee and moves over to the sink, washing it up.

How can she be so nonchalant about what she just told me?

"Listen, honey, I'm not telling you all this so you can look at me like a mirror into your future. I knew, when he passed, I knew… it was the end of our love story. But, you know, I have a feeling about a lot of things. You remember that tornado I predicted, don't you?" I nod my head vigorously because I do know. Mrs. Graham has an uncanny way of sensing things.

"I just feel like this isn't the end for you. Now, I don't want to give you false hope or anything, but I don't know. I just feel like you are gonna get more out of life." She pats my shoulder as she passes, making her way back to the front door.

She calls over her shoulder to me as she lets herself out. "Don't be hiding yourself in this house, baby. And let me know if you need more glue."

The click of the light switch and hum of the fluorescent bulbs heating up lightens my heart a little. Mrs. Graham was right, I can't hide myself in my house.

It took me the rest of the night to finish gluing Humphrey. I thought a lot about what she said. I don't think Freddy would want me to hang out on my porch, smoking in my pajamas, for the rest of my life, but it's only been a week. Well, almost two if you count from the last time I was with him. Forever, if you measure with my heart.

I decided to go to Dripping for a change of scenery. Even its name reminds me of him: Dripping for Your Pleasure. That was how he kept me when he wasn't winning over my heart.

I thought I was so clever when I named this place. Dirty and suggestive drink names with a gothy motif. I flick on the lights, waiting for the flickering I've come to expect, but they shine bright and true because it was him. The unsettling feeling of someone leaning over my shoulder had turned into the comfort of his presence, and now the lack of it is like an echo down an empty hallway. I still plan to stay closed, but maybe wiping the counters and making new menu items will be productive. My new sandwich that I'd named after him is still advertised on the chalkboard, *The Humphrey.*

I'm not going to remove it from the menu, but I want to make something new for this new phase. I start pulling out ingredients to brainstorm. What represents Freddy? What represents my feelings? I start mixing the base for cupcakes, reminiscing about the last few months I've spent with him. I don't want to make something that represents my sadness; he deserves better than that.

The sensations from my first dream come back to me. The earthy smell of sawdust, the salty taste of his sweat, mixed with the decadence of his kisses that felt like home. The comfort of his touches and how safe and hopeful he made me feel. I mix and measure, lost in my emotions.

The oven timer lets me know they're done. I set them on the counter to cool until I can add the frosting I've made. While I wait, I walk around to my chalkboard, ready to add my newest menu item, Falling for Freddy, a play on the season and my heart. A spiced gingerbread cupcake with a salted caramel cream cheese frosting and caramel drizzle.

I put the final flair on the end of the word drizzle and replace my chalk. As I turn to head back to the kitchen, movement catches my eye through the front glass. There, in front of the door to the coffee shop, sitting on the concrete, is a man. He's leaning his back to the door like he's been there for a while. His head is bowed down, and his arms resting on his knees. Someone waiting for me to open? I put a mention about the change in hours on my social media, but I hadn't come down to put a sign on the door. I should probably do that, or I'll end up with a line of frustrated customers.

I flip the lock and crack the door a bit, and he falls backward with the opening of the door. "I'm sorry, Sir, but I'm closed for—" My words catch in my throat. His face tips backward to look up at me, his beautiful eyes wide with hope and a relieved smile splitting his face. "Hello, love."

CHAPTER 20
ELYSIUM

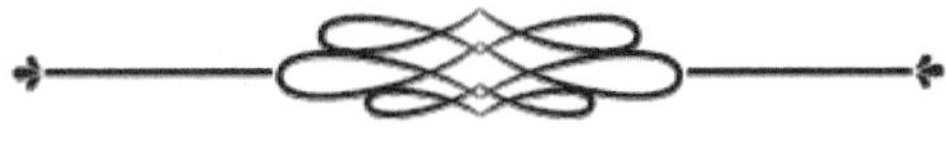

Fredrick

SCALDING WATER SPURTS FROM the showerhead. I've been alternating between suffocating him with the steam and then blasting cold water and opening the bathroom window to let in the fall night air, torturing him with the shift between sweating and freezing. Threatening him with messages on the steamed-up bathroom mirror didn't convince him to return what he'd stolen. The bane of my prolonged existence has always been that I could never move that godforsaken bottle.

If I could so much as grasp Humphrey, I would be making my way back to Willow instead of spending time with this fucker. He shivers on the tile of the bathroom floor, begging for me to stop. Why would I ever stop? If we are trapped together, let him enjoy his choices. If I can't be with her, then I'll spend the rest of my existence, however long that may be, making this piece of shit's life a torturous one.

He's pissed himself; blood, snot, and saliva mix all over his face. My anger boils and festers with every sniveling breath he takes. "YOU— WILL HAVE HELL, BECAUSE I— AM IN HELL!" I lean down and scream my scalding curses directly into his face.

I don't care that he can't hear them, with the fire in my chest, I will melt down his existence. I'm riffling drawers in the bedroom, looking for inspiration for what's to come next, when I hear voices. Male voices. As I walk up the hallway to have a look, one of them walks right through me. He shoulders in the bathroom door where Gerald is crying and hauls him out and into the living room.

Gerald can barely stand; his feet scrape along the carpet as he's dragged down the hallway. I sneer in sadistic pleasure at my craftsmanship, although it's disappointing that it will be cut short now that we have guests. I follow my new partners in torture, but am stopped short in my dark reverie when I see who else has arrived.

Willow, Krista, and some other gent I don't recognize are standing in the entryway, faced off with a group of men, one of them holding a gun. The anger that burned so fiercely before has melted into the chilling ice of fear. As much as I longed to see her again, it was never like this, with a her life being threatened by a gun in her face.

Before I can process how or why she's here or what I can do to help, Gerald finds a burst of desperate energy. He lunges for Willow and Humphrey. Chaos erupts around the living room. Krista and the other friend grab for Willow, trying to help her. Before I can jump into the fight, the movement and the glint of metal catch my eye. The gun.

My worst fears begin to play out as he raises the weapon, aiming right into the mix of limbs that make up Willow and Gerald as they scramble for control of Humphrey. There's no way he'll be able to aim for just Gerald, and my gut tells me he doesn't care. I leap forward, wrapping both of my hands around his wrist. The muscles of his arm tense under my grasp as he tries to yank free. Please, God, don't let this gun go off.

I struggle to maintain my focus, pulling all of my energy toward pushing his arm into the air and his aim away from her. His face is contorted in anger and confusion. He claws at the invisible force wrapped around his wrist, prying his fingers away from the gun.

Every scream and grunt coming from the floor threatens to pull my focus away. The other goons have spread out around the room. They try to pull Krista and their friend away from Willow and yell profane threats at Gerald. I want to help her, I want to fight for her, but the best thing I can do right now is keep this nutter from shooting her.

A scream from Willow pulls my attention away, I turn to see what's happening to her. He jerks his elbow backward, bringing his arm back down, and the gun goes off. Shooting into the ceiling, plaster and dust come cascading down. The fight on the floor freezes with the gunfire. I take a moment to glance at Willow to see if she's been hurt, still hanging onto the arm attached to the gun. That glance cost me everything. The gunman snatches Humphrey away from Gerald and smashes him onto the floor. The destroyed statue shattered along with my heart.

The anguished sound Willow makes as she tries to scoop up the fragmented pieces of Humphrey, her tormented expression, triggers a wave of raw and primitive grief in my own chest. My throat aches with defeat at the choked and desperate sobs coming from the other half of my soul while she holds the disjointed face of the impish little man that brought us together.

I would give anything to take that feeling away. I reach forward to touch her face, to let her know I'm right here, that I'll never leave her. My fingers gently brush the tear from her cheek. She raises her own hand to where she feels mine, the warmth of her skin like a balm on the raw and bleeding emotions coursing through me. Her soft cheek under my hand... then the sensation begins to fade... I begin to fade...and...

This is the third time I've experienced this. The first time was the day I drank from Humphrey. I listed in black abyss for what felt like days. The second was when Gerald stole my bottle. Though, I'm not sure how much that counts because it wasn't actually the abyss, it was the trunk of his shitty car. That one terrified me more than the first. This time, this time feels final. I can't call it peace because I can only find that with Willow. But it does feel like an end. There's no light, no sound, no sensation except the longing I have for her and the resignation that this is eternity.

My head feels like someone's taken a hammer to it. I roll to my side and fight the urge to vomit. Squeezing my eyes shut to block out the light as another heave tries to work its way up my throat. My hands grope the carpet for purchase, and the sting of something sharp bites at my palms.

Light? Touch? I open my eyes and look down at my hands. Dirty green carpet littered with splintered furniture and glass. Dark stains are splattered around the floor and walls, and the putrid smell of excrement stings my nostrils.

Gerald's apartment? I sit up and hold my aching head in my hands. The impulse to vomit is still strong. I take several slow, deep breaths and try to find the missing part of my memories. The last thing I can recall is Willow. Her eyes filled with tears, and her hurt expression as she raked something up from the floor—Humphrey!

I sit up too quickly, the room spinning and the bile rising from my stomach. I roll onto my hands and knees, trying to breathe through the nausea as I shift my hands over the carpet through the splintered furniture and shattered glass, looking for remnants of Humphrey.

It takes effort to keep my eyes open against the pounding in my head. I have to find him; he's the key to my existence. If I'm still here, Humphrey must be okay. I don't turn anything up on the living room floor. A cacophony of metal clanging and wood slamming reverberates through the apartment as I stumble around. I check all cabinets, drawers, closets, and rubbish bins. Searching as quickly as I can manage for any signs of him. This can't happen. If Humphrey is missing, then what does that mean for me? Am I trapped here? Gerald is nowhere to be found, but neither is Willow. She wouldn't have left me behind. Not again.

"Hey, mister, your apartment looks like shit," a child's voice calls from the outer hallway. I turn the corner of the living room to see a young man, maybe twelve or thirteen, standing in the hall. He looks confused and horrified by what he sees through the doorway.

"What the hell happened? You had a bad bender?" he asks. I turn in a circle, looking for who he might be talking to. But I'm the only one here. It can't be me?

"Hello... can you see me?" I wave my hands in front of me as a test.

"Duh, I can see you. Are you still tripping?" his sarcastic report is like a slap, surely not.

"How many fingers am I holding?" I lift my hands up in front of my face.

"Six," he says. Bloody hell, he can see me. I start patting myself down, still unsure if it's real. Forgetting the kid, I rush back toward the bathroom and check the mirror. A face I haven't seen reflected in decades looks back at me. Holy fuck! I can see myself!

This stair well smells of piss, but I take a deep inhale all the same. Breathing in freedom. The hazy sky indicates late afternoon, it will be dark sooner than I can blink. Turning about, I try to find any indication of street names or directions. The signs here are dilapidated. If there is a street sign, the lettering is deteriorated. Chilling wind cuts through my sweater. It's exhilarating. The setting sun, the weight of my legs on my feet. The haze of my imprisoned self is lifted, and I feel so... ALIVE!

How do I find Willow, though? I've no experience navigating around the city. On our outings to the library, I was so focused on her I didn't really take in the landscape, not that it would help much here. I decided to walk in the direction of the street lamps, hands in the pockets of my trousers. An eerie sense of déjà vu settles in my gut. The last time I went walking down a sidewalk was the day my life changed. And now, my life is changing again. Only this time, it's for the better.

As it turns out, not many people are interested in giving directions to a stranger dressed from the 1930's. I look and speak differently, and I clearly have no idea where anything is in this city. Some have tried giving me landmarks as a reference, to no avail, street names— meaningless. Finally, they'll point in a general direction to get me started.

I can't even be certain that the address I remember from the coffee shop window is even accurate. I sat next to a tree and waited out the night. When the dawn broke, I started on my journey again. A lovely woman feeding crows at a park I passed shared her bench with me. She'd never heard of Dripping for Your Pleasure, but said it sounded like a place I'd fit in.

I've walked all day, gotten lost numerous times, but I finally found my destination. Like a beacon guiding me in from the sea, a blood red door with glass facing, the painted styled script with the words...Dripping for Your Pleasure, the Spookiest Coffee Shop in Town. It's sunset, and the golden hue of the sky casts a romantic glow over the storefront. The lights are off. I press my face into the glass and cup my hands around my eyes, searching for any sign she might be inside. I'm so close, but not yet at my destination. I won't have peace until I have her in my arms. I turn and lean my back against the door and slide down to the sidewalk. I'll sit and wait until she returns.

Hhuuuuuu, my neck is cramped and my forehead aches from resting on my crossed arms. My arse is numb too. I have been practicing what I'll say when I see her again. I have a full speech about how our love transcends time and life itself. About how I'll be the perfect partner and all the promises I can make to ensure her eternal happiness.

I'm lost in these thoughts when suddenly, the door jerks backward, and I go with it. Looking up into the face of the most beautiful soul in the universe, all my poetic words seem inadequate compared to the emotion I feel when I look deep into her eyes. All I can muster is, "Hello, love."

The door was the only thing that kept me partially upright. When it's jerked back the rest of the way, I go smacking right down on my back, nearly cracking my head open on the tile floor of the coffee shop entrance. Willow takes several cautious steps backward, disbelief pants her face. She's shaking her head and clutching at her hair, her eyes glass over, and tears trickle down her cheeks.

"Sweetheart, don't cry. Please don't cry. I'm so sorry…" I reach out for her, but she steps away again. "I'm so sorry, Willow. I never would have left if I could have controlled it—" I'm then attacked by a mass of blonde hair and arms. A strangling embrace that slams me back flat on the floor.

I roll us over so I can pull her body into mine, and I hold her as I've longed to from the moment I laid eyes on her. I hold her as if I could absorb her into myself so we would never be parted for any reason ever again. I hold her in an embrace that I hope speaks all the words I'll never find to properly express my connection to her, because simply saying "I love you" will never be enough.

"I have you, now. I really have you… my sweetheart. Not death, not time… not even magic can keep me from you." I whisper gently in her ear as she cries into my chest. Her hands clawing at my sweater as if she fears I'll vanish right from beneath her again.

The memory of her grieved wailing as Humphrey smashed to the floor echoes in my mind, and my heart cracks with hers. Elation and heartache intertwine. "I know, my love, I know. I know." I whisper over and over. Reassuring her that I feel it too. The desperation. The gut-wrenching grief at what was almost lost. The rapture of having her in my arms again. It's like I have risen from the dead. I've finally passed on into my next existence. This is my Elysium. She is my Elysium.

The day has long passed into the dark of evening, but it feels like only seconds ago I finally got Willow back into my arms. We've lain here on the floor of her coffee shop, both unwilling to leave the other's embrace. We need it like we need air.

I pet her head, lacing my fingers tenderly through the strands of blonde silk. Coffee and cream, sweet vanilla, and sugar. I lean my face down toward the top of her head and take a deep inhale. Holding it in my lungs for as long as I can, hoping to permeate my insides with her. Her fingers have finally relaxed around my sweater, but she hasn't spoken a word. "It's real, Willow. I'm real." I try to reassure her. She answers by wrapping her arms around my chest and squeezing me even closer to her.

Realization hits me, I've held her many times. But this is the first time she has really held me. Held me and been able to truly feel me, the warmth of our bodies mixing. Her head lifts, leaving the skin of my neck cold in the absence of her breath there. Red, tearful eyes search mine for answers. I don't know that I have any. But I'll take the result no matter. She lifts her hand to my face, grazing the stubble that's grown my jaw. Hair that hasn't grown in decades. Her thumb caresses the corner of my lips. I part them to kiss the tip. A fresh tear frees itself from the corner of her eye. "So, many tears for me, love?" I whisper.

"I can't believe I'm looking at you right now," she whispers. Her eyes trace the lines of my face; her fingertip brushes the tips of my eyelashes and down my cheekbone. My eyes close at the gentle and loving sensation of her touches. I take another deep inhale of her coffee and cream scent. Catching me a little off guard, she dives forward and crashes her mouth to mine, her kisses deep and urgent. Full of all the emotions we can't properly put into words. I tangle my hands into her hair at the base of her skull and press her to me as I open my mouth to hers, inviting in all of her passion and neediness.

Tugging her hair, I lift her head to gain access to her neck, laving at her skin like I could devour her if I tried. Her breath warms my ear as she exhales in pleasure. The skin of her back is so smooth and soft under my palm as I run my hand underneath her t-shirt.

I need to touch her skin. I need her skin all over my skin. I pull her shirt over her head, but before I can go for her bra, she is pulling at my sweater. I was dressed in my best clothing the day I disappeared; it's entirely too many layers. Sweater, necktie, dress shirt... I pull the center of her bra and snap the fabric open. Pressing into her, I'm blessed with her soft, pillowy breasts against my chest.

I wrap my arms around her ribcage and press my hands into her back between her shoulder blades and up the back of her neck, holding her to me as I run my mouth over her collarbone. She clings to me in return, we are desperate for each other. Shifting my body, one arm wrapped around her back still and the other hand pulling her thigh around my waist as I press my thickened cock into her center.

She moans in response and squeezes her leg around my hips and ass to keep me in place. Undulating her pelvis into my hips in time with me, my fingers dig into the soft of her thigh, and my mouth moves down her chest to devour her tender breast. I suck and lave at her nipple, burying my nose into the fat of her breast. Her hand slips up the back of my head, and her fingers pull at my hair. I love the pain. The smell and taste of her skin, the feel of her, the feel of me pressed into her... It's like I've woken from a world of black and white into a vibrant kaleidoscope of sensation. Everything is more powerful, more radiant than before.

Our frantic hands relieve each other of the remainder of our clothing. The cool tile floor of the coffee shop sends goose bumps over my skin. My muscles tense in anticipation of this moment. I roll to my back as Willow, my Willow, steps over my legs and lowers her body to mine. My hands find her hips to help her descent. Running up the course of her body to reverently trace the curves of her breasts and back down over her ass cheeks and thighs. I gently coax her to lift her hips and allow me entrance. Our eyes locked in the longing gaze of two souls finally united. My breath catching in my lungs as she glides down onto me.

Her hands braced on my chest, mine on her hips. We glide together in slow, intimate undulations, her warmth and wet wrapping me up, a haven to bury myself for the rest of time. "Willow, I," I gasp out her name like a prayer. Pulling her down to me, I band my arms around her back and hold her body close as I grind myself upward into her. She gasps and grunts until she cums with her face buried into the base of neck and I follow her over that edge into the blissful abyss. We're both shaking, sweat slicking our skin. I move her hair back from her forehead and kiss her tenderly. The unspoken 'I love you' hanging between our gaze.

Willow sits on the cool stainless-steel countertop, still completely naked, hand feeding me the most delicious spiced cupcake with caramel frosting. I stand snug between her thighs, also still naked. I've been alternating between eating her treats and her pussy for the last hour.

"This is so unsanitary," she giggles.

"I promise, love, I will help scrub every inch of this place for you," I say as I take another cupcake from the plate and use it to spread frosting over her nipples. I'm bowing my head to taste-test them when the jiggle of a door handle breaks the silence. Alarmed, Willow pulls me to her and wraps her arms and legs around me. Cupcake smashes into the back of my head, and the frosting on her nipples smears across both our chests. "Willow? I saw your car out back. You in here, babe?"

Our heads whip in the direction of the back door to see Krista turn the corner into the kitchen and scream. "Ah! What the hell, Willow! Who the fuck is this?"

"Uh, hey Krista, uh, meet Freddy."

CHAPTER 21
EPILOGUE

Willow

SHRRRFV, SHRRRFV, SHRRRFV. THE rhythm is steady. The persistent sounds of hands at work drift from the garage. Light glows ahead of me from the hanging bulb in the ceiling, casting a shadow of a man. He rocks his body with the movement of the sound, forward and back. The smell of sawdust and wood stain tingle my nose. I fight to stifle a sneeze, but I fail. "You always think you can sneak up on me, sweetling." He lets a half grin slip but doesn't look up from his work. I take the opportunity to slip a little closer.

He's shirtless and sweaty, his jeans hanging low on his hips, they're smeared with dirt and stains. He wipes his hands with a rag, then his neck and forehead. "If you keep interrupting me, I'll never finish these pieces." He's purposefully avoiding looking at me, but I catch the twitch at the corner of his mouth.

I clasp my hands behind my back and stretch my chest upward as I bounce on my tiptoes. "Uh, you know how I feel about that move." He slaps the rag down on his workbench and turns to face me, his grin now fully spread over his handsome face. Freddy spreads his warm palms around my naked waist and leans down toward my chest. "You two are nothing but trouble," he says to my breasts and gives them each a firm kiss. He rises and rubs his hands down each of my ass cheeks as he presses his lips to mine.

"You know, in order to have a successful custom furniture business, I do actually have to make the furniture." He kisses the tip of my nose and pulls my body flush to his. The sweat on his chest is sticky on my skin. "I know, but you're just so irresistible when you're all sweaty, and your muscles are bulging, and that one wavy lock of hair is falling into your eye..." I trace my finger down the center of his chest and try to look adorable.

"Hmmm, I think I have a solution to your distractions, though," he says as he reaches up to take my wrists in his hands. He pulls me deeper into the garage toward the back wall. He gathers something metal from the workbench as we pass it. Turning me so I'm now standing in front of him, he caresses my breasts and continuing down my belly, kissing my neck behind my ear. He distracts me as he slips something soft over my wrists. I lift my right hand to inspect the padded leather cuff.

While I'm busy trying to put together what he's done, Freddy clips a stretch of metal chain to the cuffs and threads it through hooks in the overhead support beam. He pulls the chains, lifting my hands overhead. "Freddy!" I tug on my wrists to no avail. I'm stuck. He smacks my bare ass with a loud pop.

"There, now you'll be kept out of trouble while I finish sanding this table." He turns away from me and saunters his fine ass back over to his work station.

"You are diabolical, Freddy." I try my best to look affronted, but it isn't convincing, and I know it. He looks too good leaning over his work.

He pretends to ignore me while he meticulously inspects the already perfectly smooth tabletop that he's been building. He smooths his hand over the surface and gives it two hard smacks. Smacks I feel right on my ass. "Yep, she's a thing of beauty." He rounds the table, cleaning his hands again with the rag. Slowly approaching me, he eyes me up and down as I wiggle in my restraints, my thighs slippery with anticipation.

"Now, what to do with this naughty little distraction?" He leans in closely, almost touching his lips to mine. His finger sliding through my slick pussy.

"Mmmm, did you enjoy the show, love?" He rubs his finger around my clit and it feels so good. "Yes," I whisper.

"What were you looking for when you decided to come down to my workshop naked, Willow?" he asks.

"I was looking for a large, solid piece of wood, Freddy." I counter.

"Hmmm, is that why you fell in love with a carpenter, Willow?" He licks up the column of my throat.

"No, but it does have its advantages," I say.

I shriek as he slaps my ass hard. "Sassy, girl, you are."

He unfastens his belt and pants. I wiggle excitedly. Freddy loops his arms under my thighs, causing me to shriek again as I'm lifted into the air. He rubs his hard cock through my wetness then notches the tip at my entrance. "Do your arms hurt, love?" he asks with sincerity. I know he would never want me to be uncomfortable.

"No, I'm good. Don't stop." I wiggle my hips to try and help things along. I can't get enough of this man. He grins back at me and slams his cock home.

"Oh!" I can't keep the smile off my face. The stretch, the force, God, he feels so good. I undulate my hips trying to get friction on my clit while he teases me by not moving. He tries to act like he's in charge, but I know he is just as crazy about me as I am about him. He begins to thrust and the swinging motion created from my precarious dangling creates a rhythm of pleasure so intense. Knowing I'm naked in the garage and someone could walk up to the driveway and see us adds an element of risk. Krista has probably bleached her eyeballs from how often she's caught us.

He picks up his pace, slamming into me like a piston, hard, with purpose, reverberating through my entire body. I'm screaming his name and incoherent praises as my body convulses with pleasure. The metal clinking of the chains pulsates in time with his thrusting. "Ah, fuck, Willow!" he cums on a roar, hot cum painting my insides.

Freddy unhooks the wrist straps and lowers me to his workbench, using his shirt as a blanket for me to sit on. "Did you seriously put those hooks up there so you could chain me up?" I ask. He laughs and says, "No, I put those hooks up there because I built you a porch swing. I thought you could sit and read or draw while I worked. It's just my fortune that they have more than one purpose." He grins at me as he pulls a tarp off a large object on the floor. It's a beautifully crafted swing with cup holders in the armrest, framed out to leave room for a large cushion.

"Maybe we could put some pillows and a blanket on it for you?" He looks back at me, waiting for my reaction. He's worked so hard trying to create a custom furniture business. When he told me it had been his dream before, I pushed him to try and go for it. He's gotten quite the following, there's a mile long list of commissions to fill, and has even put a few smaller artistic pieces in Jolie's shop. I don't know when he would have had time to make a whole ass swing. And it's for me?

"It's beautiful, thank you so much, Freddy," I say.

He's really adjusted well to modern life. There was a lot he'd learned as an observer for decades that helped, but also a lot he didn't know. A few heart attacks and ten traffic violations later, he's finally learned how to drive. Jolie's fiancé and his team were able to get Freddy the documents he needed to look like a typical citizen. I'm so grateful for them, and for their blind acceptance of my previously-ghost-boyfriend.

He helps out at the coffee shop during the week and works on his furniture business on the weekends and evenings. He's outgrowing this garage, though. We'll soon need to look at getting his own space. I'm lost in thought about possible locations when I notice that Freddy's standing in front of me, staring intently. A shadow of worry briefly crosses his face. "Are you happy, Willow? Do I make you happy?"

"Fredrick Hughes, you know that I am. I am crazy about you." I say, unsure of where this doubt is coming from. Then I see it. On the tip of his index finger. A small gold band with a delicate diamond. He lifts his arm, holding the ring between us.

"This belonged to my mother. It's the only belonging of my parents I ever had. I know it's small, but it would honor me so much if you'd wear it, if you'd agree to one day be my wife?" He searches my eyes beseechingly. I can't believe it, his family heirloom, that he would give me something so precious. I touch his finger where the ring rests. It's beautiful, so delicate. I look up at his face and search his eyes. How did I get so lucky?

"Freddy, you are everything to me. I can't imagine a future without you right here with me. Of course, I would be your wife." I reach for his face, bringing him closer so I can kiss him tenderly. He breaks our embrace and stares at me for a beat. "I have carried this ring for decades. It was a cruel reminder of the life I could have had, but thought I never would. Now, it feels like happily ever after." He slides it onto my finger, then laces his fingers with mine.

I gaze down at our hands intertwined, and know that he's absolutely right. It does feel like happily ever after.

Fredrick

My shoes squeak on the freshly mopped linoleum. I rub my sweaty palms down the front of my jumper, then shove them in my pockets. Everything smells fresh and clean here. The hallways are decorated bright and cheery.

"Relax, would you?" Willow says. She slips her arm through mine and leads me down the hallway. I try to take a calming breath while we wait to be buzzed in through the large automatic doors. Bile rises from my gut, and my heart feels like it's one beat from bursting out of my chest. We cross the threshold of the entryway leading into a large common room. Willow gives my arm a gentle tug. There, at the back table, quietly working a puzzle, is Edith Grant. I couldn't believe it when Willow told me she was still alive and stashed away in a poor facility.

Thank God for Willow's friends. Jolie's fiancé and his men, Lawrence and Davis. Without them, I'm not sure how we could have moved Edith to a better home. Honestly, they've done more for us than I could ever repay. I was able to get authentic documents like a birth certificate and a Social Security card. They also dug up some seedy dealings on that bastard lawyer that Willow's mother tried to set her up with. It was juicy enough to merit a payout that will keep Edith in this top-of-the-line care facility dedicated to individuals with dementia and Alzheimer's Disease.

The exits are all made to look like bookshelves from the inside, and the private rooms face a centralized common area where residents can participate in leisure activities or do supervised cooking with the staff. Everything is set up to make them feel like they are staying in a cozy home, not a nursing facility.

I fidget with my clothing, tugging at the collar of my shirt. "Okay, so everyone here thinks I'm her granddaughter, and I'm gonna introduce you as my fiancé, got it?" Willow whispers in my ear. I nod my head as I continue to look onward. What if she recognizes me? What if it upsets her? "Maybe this was a mistake. I don't want to agitate her." I start to pull back, regretting the decision to come here.

"Stop that, you needed to see that she was okay. I think you should talk to her. It's gonna be fine, I promise." She tries to reassure me. Before I can argue any more, we're approached by one of the nurses, who ushers us over to Edith's table. "Edith, honey, look. You have visitors. You're sweet granddaughter has come back to see you." She pulls a chair out for Willow right next to Edith. I walk around the table and take a seat directly in front of her.

Edith beams at Willow and pats her hand. "Oh, it's so nice to see you. Do you like puzzles?" she asks. "Yes, I love puzzles. Can we work on this one together for a little while?" Willow turns her eyes to me and tries to give me a reassuring smile. I hold my breath waiting to be noticed. Edith gives me a warm smile and gestures toward the strewn puzzle pieces on the table.

That's it. We work in comfortable silence together for about an hour, then accompany Edith on a stroll through the little rose garden that connects back to the common room. I trail behind Edith and Willow. I'm not sure what I had hoped to accomplish today. On the surface, I told myself it was just to see her, to know she was happy and well in her new home. If I dig deeper, though, a small part of me hoped she'd remember. The last connection to my old life.

It's gone four o'clock now, and visiting hours are ending. I gently wrap my arm around Edith's shoulder and give her a little hug goodbye. She looks up at me with a curious expression for just a moment.

"Don't I know you?" she asks. Warmth spreads through my chest.

"Yes, I'm Willow's fiancé, Freddy," I say and smile down at her.

"Oh, yes, of course." She pats my arm like we are old friends. And of course we are.

Edith, London 1935

I slip through the aisles of my shop, searching for the place that feels proper. Another parcel arrived from my parents today. This time, they are touring again in Eastern Europe. As with every stop, they send me some "treasure" they hope will assuage their long years of absence in my life.

Dearest Edith,

Your father and I do miss you so, as always. While walking the market in Denmark, we found this fascinating little man. The stall holder is from Eastern Germany, and she told us this bottle has been in her family for generations.

It's very special, Edith, and has magical properties, so please handle it with care. When she said it could cure anything, I knew I had to send it to you, my darling girl. I do worry about you, so when we are apart...

I didn't bother to finish reading the letter. They all end the same way. Justification of her guilt for leaving behind a daughter she wasn't interested in to a line of governesses.

When the gifts took over the house, it was too glaring for them to face when they came home to visit me. The piles of evidence of how disconnected they were from their only daughter. So, I was gifted my shop. A museum of reminders for every missed birthday or childhood milestone.

I've enjoyed some of the gifts, but I've sold most of them. Even after all this time, I've never run short of inventory. I squeeze between the shelves and round the corner where the mounted boar's head— a memento from one of father's hunting trips in France— hangs on the wall.

I've placed every item in here with intention. Letting its energy guide me. Someone will walk this path through the shop and find something they need, something they are fated to have. That's how I've reconciled the collection of these worldwide artifacts. As if I'm doing a service for the universe.

Stopping at an empty space on the shelf, it feels right to place him here. "There you are, friend, a new home until you become someone's perfect find."

Acknowledgements

A big gigantic thank you to my friends and family who have put up with me and helped me through this journey.

Thank you to my parents, who have given their unconditional support of their well mannered southern daughter becoming a smut author.

Thank you to my brother, you have been there with me every step of this journey. Thank you for encouraging me not to stop at one book. You have talked me through the imposter syndrome and the excitement. Couldn't do this without you.

A funny story about why book 2 of this series is a paranormal romance. While I was visiting my brother, who lives out of state, get took me to this amazing second hand store. That is where we found Humphrey. On a final pass through before checking out we spotted him a on shelf. We literally felt like he appeared out of nowhere because we had already combed the store. He was a "perfect find" for my brother so of course he was coming home with us.

While getting wrapped up, the store clerk told us Humphrey was actually a wine decanter. I jokingly told my brother, "Don't open it, your luck you'll bring home a poltergeist." And that is how the story of Willow and Freddy began.

Thank you also to some very special friends, Crystal and Megan. Thank you for all your help with test reads, editing, and cheering me on as this story developed. Thank you for being the kind of friends I can trust with a project so dear to my heart. And thank you for still being able to look me in the face after the nasty things I wrote in this book.

To everyone who has encouraged me, thank you so much for being with me on this journey. I love you all so much.

About the Author

J.P. Newmon was born and raised in Louisiana. She is a lover of all forms of art and enjoys photography, drawing, painting, and multimedia work in addition to writing. Her debut novel, Training Sweet Jolie: Book 1 of the Dirty Voyeurs series, released in January of 2025, and she looks forward to many works to follow. Romance by JP is a unique blend of authentic emotional journey and shockingly spicy intimacy. Her love for reading and the romance genre is what inspired her to take the leap from reader to self-published author. When she isn't writing romance, she is kept busy being a mom and working full-time.

Need more JP Newmon?

Follow @JPNewmonauthor on various social media platforms

Visit her website https://jpnewmonauthor.com/and sign up for her newsletter to get updates and previews on upcoming projects.

ALSO BY J.P. NEWMON

If you enjoyed Willow and Freddy's story then you may also want
to check out Book 1 in the Dirty Voyeurs series.
Training Sweet Jolie: Dirty Voyeurs Book 1

Coming Next
Bound and Exposed: Dirty Voyeurs Book 3
(Krista's story)
Tales for Bedtime: Erotic Short Stories to Help You Fall Asleep